11-82

X

Douglas, Ellen

A lifetime burning

C1982.

DATE			

82
83
84
81

92
00

© THE BAKER & TAYLOR CO.

A
Lifetime
Burning

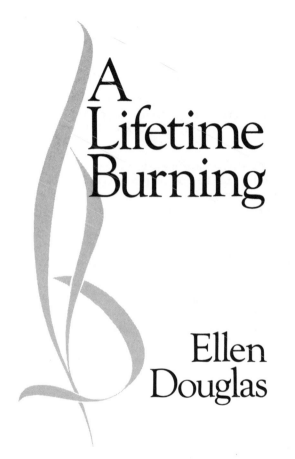

A Lifetime Burning

Ellen Douglas

Random House
New York

Grateful acknowledgment is made to Harcourt Brace Jovanovich, Inc.,
and Faber & Faber Ltd., London, for permission to reprint an excerpt from
"East Coker" in *Four Quartets;* copyright 1943, by T. S. Eliot, renewed,
1971, by Esme Valerie Eliot. Reprinted by permission of the publishers.

Library of Congress Cataloging in Publication Data
Douglas, Ellen, pseud.
  A lifetime burning.
  I. Title.
PS3554.O825L5   1982   813'.54   82–40141
ISBN 0–394–52719–4

Manufactured in the United States of America

98765432

First Edition

Home is where one starts from. As we grow older
The world becomes stranger, the pattern more complicated
Of dead and living. Not the intense moment
Isolated, with no before and after,
But a lifetime burning in every moment
And not the lifetime of one man only
But of old stones that cannot be deciphered.

—T. S. ELIOT, *Four Quartets*

A
Lifetime
Burning

Monday Aug. 4th

I've put it off, sometimes easily, without even thinking, sometimes painfully, sometimes believing I was not putting it off at all, for—how long? Six months? Six years? Thirty years?

There are so many things you can do to take up the time until the day is over. Everyone has his own kind of thing, whether it's pulling grass from between the bricks or going through the car wash or putting up pickles or scrubbing the outside of the house; or, if you like competition, playing bridge or tennis; or, if you like idleness and unconsciousness, fishing or getting drunk.

Of the last four I like only fishing and getting drunk, and these only while I'm doing it. I like to hold the drink in my hand, move into the euphoria of drunkenness; and I like to feel the jerk of the bream on the hook, admire his glittering body, add him to the stringer. But I don't like cleaning fish and after I get drunk feel guilty, even if I don't have a hangover. The feeble old Methodist God still easily holds me by the throat (I'm feebler, too), twists my arm, gives me a toothache or a kick in the breasts.

Put off what? For one thing, trying to understand. That's what I tell myself I'll do. I'll sit down at my desk with a pen I like and a stack of the lined paper with five holes in the side like we used in high school, and . . .

Tuesday Aug. 5th

No. Yes. No.

The usual ruses today. Should I turn on the TV and do my sit-ups and ride the stationary bike while I watch Donahue?

No.

I find myself outside starting the sprinkler on the caladiums. If I can putter a little longer, the time I have allotted for writing will be over for today.

No.

I am a teacher of literature and ordinarily I would be dressing by now to go to the college to meet a class or keep office hours, shifting into a frame of mind that excludes my personal life; but this summer I chose not to teach during the second summer-school session. The need for ruses, for time fillers, is partly the result, I suppose, of this unusual idleness, and so, perhaps, is the decision to try to say—*something*.

The weather this summer has been hot even for the Deep South. It has not rained for twenty-three days. Now and then in the still afternoon heat a limb tears loose from its trunk with a ripping, crackling groan and comes crashing down. Is it the drought? Or is it from a general statewide drop in the water table caused by the draining of swamps and the "speeding of floods to the sea," as one brochure from the U.S. Army Corps of Engineers puts it?

I drag the pieces of the limb into the garden cart and haul them back to the woodpile. George (my husband) can saw them up later. He likes to saw—it's a welcome gross motor activity after hours of stitching together eyelids or torn pieces of gut. Green moss and shriveled resurrection ferns still cling to the bark of one of the limbs—this one from an oak. The crashing sycamore limb has brought down with it one from the neighboring live oak tree. The inside wood is dry, punky, hardly worth hauling to the woodpile.

But, as you see, I am now back at my table, writing, the blue thread of ink raveling across the page.

This observation may be true: Even writing may be a way of putting off. I don't know what to write and I put down whatever word comes next into my head.

I want to say everything at once, to understand, to accept, to stop striving. Also, I want to say—nothing. Or, to put it

Here's a measure I took a year or two ago, which I believed was the reverse of putting off: I tried Senoi dreaming.

A nutty friend of Corinne's—a very decent if troubled young man who has an M.S. in clinical psychology and is now a plumbing contractor—had given me a monograph called "Senoi Dreamwork," about a people in the Malaysian archipelago, of whom every man, woman, and child has as his profession, from the time he can talk, dreaming and the interpretation of dreams. These people listen to the voices of the spirits good and evil who wander through their sleep, capture and learn to control them, elicit their advice and support—and then they make artworks or search for natural objects to remind them of what they have learned. They live, as it were, in museums of the unconscious. And they are extraordinarily "well-adjusted." They smile at one another and at visitors, fish and labor in their fields with great pleasure, engage in random adolescent sex, ceremoniously lend out their husbands and wives (both, without prejudice), and never punish their children. They do not go insane or commit violent crimes.

The monograph explains their technique of dreaming and interpreting dreams, and one painful day—that was the winter I read *The Families of Schizophrenics, Beyond Games and Scripts, More Joy of Sex,* and *The Story of O.*—I decided to try it.

To do it right, you must lie down and invite a kind of semiconscious fantasy state; then you must identify the "leading figure" in the fantasy, who may be either a good or an evil spirit, and, asleep or half asleep, seize him, hold on to him, and ask him to identify himself and to give you a "gift." (I say "him" but of course the leading figure may be female.)

I've always had a certain control over my dreams, able to command myself to dream of a particularly attractive man or to go back to sleep and finish a dream interrupted by a crying child, able to give the dream the shape of a story; and

7

the second or third time I tried Senoi dreaming it worked.

This is my dream: I am going to Colorado with my younger son James and my grandmother, also named Corinne, as am I. James is driving. We are traveling a narrow two-lane road that follows the curves of a river up into the mountains; on one side the road drops off to the riverbed, on the other the mountain rises steeply up. Everything here is wild and beautiful—veined and slaty cliffs on the left and, below us on the right, the clear, shallow, aspen-bordered river, rushing over its rocky bed.

Oh, I've driven those roads beside water often in my dreams —and in my waking fantasies, too. You stop the car, pull off on a shoulder, climb down to the water's edge, and under a sheltering overhang, invisible from above, you sit on a mossy bank in the shade of a tree that thrusts out of a crack in the rocks. Here is the place to drink wine with friends, to receive lovers, to conceive babies.

But to continue, the road narrows to one lane; piles of rubble block the freshly graded shoulder on the cliff side, as if work is being done to widen it. James drives skillfully, but we know, without telling each other, that we will come to a dead end, and we do. On our left is the steep mountainside, on our right the river—we haven't room even to turn the car around. Ahead, where the road should continue, a broad, shallow flight of gray stone stairs rises toward the mountain top. We cannot see the end of it for the mist and overhanging trees. We get out of the car, all three of us. My grandmother, who seems to be about eighty, although in fact she died at ninety when my son was a baby, is tall, still willing herself erect, thin to emaciation, so fragile I hardly dare take her arm for fear I may break it; James, a grown man, in his middle twenties, sturdy, barrel-chested, with his father's sensitive lips and wavy chestnut hair, looks at us out of brown eyes full of pain and understanding. With his help we begin to climb the stairs. I am thinking that my grandmother can't possibly make it to the top—wherever that is. We can't see it for the mists above us. She gives me a wry smile, as if she had heard me speak, and takes another

8

step. Under my hand, the bone of her forearm is narrow as a pencil, bends like a broomstraw.

At this point, half-waking, I follow the instructions in the monograph. I address James as the main figure in the dream. There is no need to capture him or to ask his name, as I might have to do if he were an evasive or an evil or an unknown figure.

"Have you a gift for me?"

"Yes," he says. He climbs down to the edge of the beautiful clear tumbling roaring river, picks up a green stone from the water, and brings it to me.

I woke up. In the middle of the night, in the darkness, I got up, unlocked the side door that opens from our bedroom into the dog yard, and went out. By the steps, not far from the small double-hinged dog door set into the bedroom wall, there is an old dense-leaved laurel tree festooned with ivy and pearled with sap where the borers have attacked it; and beside it, a pile of rocks we've found here and there over the years. One is greenish, veined with white, a little larger than my two fists. I picked it up and brought it into the house and, the next morning, scrubbed it with a stiff-bristled vegetable brush (the dog urinates daily on these rocks; it's his favorite spot) and put it on my desk.

I was uplifted. I looked at the stone on my desk and was sure if I was patient it would reveal its significance to me. And I thought the stone dream would be the first of many. I would lie every night with my eyes closed and dream my way to clarity, understanding, peace, fulfillment . . .

But instead I went to bed and did what I was supposed to do to invite the dream state, and nothing happened. No more gifts.

Later

Let me tell you about the dog. I hate the dog—and not irrationally, either. He's an Airedale, a breed noted for its ill-temper and churlishness. He barks indiscriminately at friend and foe. He has been known to knock children off their bicycles. He is vicious in his attacks on smaller dogs, cowardly toward large ones. But George loves him. If George were to die tomorrow, if I woke up in bed beside him and found him cold and dead of a heart attack (not likely: he's very healthy), it might be that the first thing I would do, before I called the children or my closest friend, or the undertaker, would be to get dressed, put the dog on his leash, get in the car, take him to the vet's, and have him destroyed.

No, I wouldn't do that. I'd be getting ready to do it when I would realize how suspicious it would look, if anybody caught me at it. For example, if I went home afterwards and called the doctor and the undertaker and it turned out that George had been dead five or six hours and somebody—the doctor's wife —had seen me at the vet's. They might decide I'd killed him —George, I mean. Otherwise, why am I out there at the vet's with the dog, cool as a cucumber?

And I would never kill George. I love him. I am content to imagine him dead.

I would never kill anybody. I could shoot the dog in a minute, if I couldn't get him to the vet's, but I would never kill a human being.

Well, of course, there are circumstances . . . Your mother is in excruciating pain with terminal cancer and you give her the bottle of Dilaudid. Or your child is attacked. But I mean, out of my own rage and hate. I wouldn't.

But I've often thought that I could go out in the backyard and get the ax—I like to chop kindling, although I'm not good at it: five-seven, not particularly muscular, and sixty-two years old—and chop the posts off the bed we sleep in. Chop it into splinters. I'd like to do that. But I wouldn't. I would never do that, either.

We bought the bed for a wedding present to ourselves. Four of the five children were conceived in it—we got one, I think, on a trip to Chicago where George did a seminar on bone marrow transplants or some such thing. All were born from it.

With Corinne, my water broke and soaked the mattress as I lay sleeping. We barely got to the hospital before she popped out.

I came home to it weeping when I lost the twins, lay sleepless in it night after night when my mother died.

We've slept in it now thirty-two years. Is it possible? Can we have been married thirty-two years?

Or, he's slept in it. Some years I wander the house, sleep on sofas, on the floor, in some other room.

The bed is sturdy, Early American, maple, the short posts topped with small removable finials shaped like penises. The inept carver meant them to be urns. Or maybe he didn't. Anyhow, you could wash the dust off, put a little vaseline on them, and use them to masturbate . . .

They're not shaped at all like penises. They're elongated urns. Still . . . You could, although it wouldn't be ideal.

I would like to find a way to tell the truth.

"Ye shall know the truth and the truth . . ." etc.

"Oh, what a tangled web we weave . . ." etc.

God knows that's the truth. The problem is, how not to deceive—oneself, everyone.

It doesn't matter.

It does matter.

In any case I have begun.

It may be that this liquid, drying blue thread making itself under my hand is the thread that holds the balloon of my head, full of helium or hydrogen or hot air, and keeps it from floating up into the sunny morning, up, up, until the heat of the sun and the difference between inside and outside pressure are too much for the thin, taut skin and it goes blam. No more balloon.

The thread is tied to a doorknob or the bedpost and the balloon (my head) is bumping and shifting against the wall and ceiling of the kitchen or of my bedroom. The thread unrolls across the page, longer and longer, the balloon escapes through a conveniently open window—I must have taken the screen out—and rises and rises until . . . Blam. Dispersed. Not so bad.

11

I will stop now. Begin again tomorrow. I could begin: It's worth doing, isn't it? Trying to tell the truth?

Thursday Aug. 7th

The way to do it, I believe, is to tell as straight as I can what's been happening. Where shall I begin? That's the question.

I believe I should begin a little more than three years ago when he turned away. There had been times when he had turned away before, even in the early years, for a couple of weeks, for a month; once, after his father died, for three months—or maybe it was longer. That was a nightmare I thought he might not wake from, and I didn't expect him to be wanting to fuck.

What to say first? I suppose that like all people we were and are strangers to each other—more so than some, perhaps, less than others.

I was raised to believe that a man's sexuality, like his self-esteem, is so fragile that you must protect it at all costs. Also I'm vain. And what else? A pitiful creature. If he didn't want me, I didn't want him to try to pretend he did. So I told myself; but I must have meant several other things as well. That was in those lost years when I—or somebody—should have been admiring my body more.

But that's way back. This new turning away lasted. One month. Two months. Six months. Now what?

And then, when the dam broke and I said, "For Christ's sake, what's the matter with me?" and we tried again, he was impotent.

Impotent, my foot. He didn't want me, that's the truth of the matter. But I thought he was impotent. He allowed me to think so. The old ruses. He complained of prostate pain. I tried to get him to see somebody. He prescribed for himself or said he had.

What can you do with a fifty-seven-year-old husband—yes, he's two years younger than I am—who won't fuck, or can't fuck? You've been married twenty-eight years. You've made five children together, buried two—twins, carried full term, born dead—and had one miscarriage. You've lived in the house together, held everything in common all those years. And you yourself are fifty-nine, eight years past the menopause. What do you do? Is it his fault he can't get it up? No, it isn't.

But it's his fault he won't talk to you about it.

I thought it would be better to leave than to keep on living in that weird cheek-by-jowl strangeness. But go where? Do what?

Oh, I knew I could make a living. As I've said, I'm a teacher and I can always make a living. But step off into loneliness? Give up my caladiums? My grassy bricks?

Besides, you don't leave your fifty-seven-year-old husband, father of your children, grandfather of your first grandchild, because he's impotent, even if he won't talk to you about it, even if he seems profoundly unaware of your rage and anguish and bafflement. He, you tell yourself, must be suffering far more than you. Cherish him. Be patient.

And there's this. I like him. I like to live with him. We have always, even when I hated him, gotten along well.

So that's how it went for a while.

There was one scene, one moment when I knew what he felt toward me.

Let me say first that he always used to tell me how clothes look on me, what to wear. I have great difficulty choosing clothes for myself because I don't know what I look like. I gaze in the mirror—I recognize myself. I turn sideways and examine myself. Am I ravishing or ridiculous?

Last summer—digression within digression—when I was visiting my older son William and his house caught fire (more about the fire later), all my clothes were burned up. For a couple of days I wore old clothes of his—his bedroom wasn't destroyed. He's slender and only an inch or two taller than I. But then I had—I thought—to get some respectable clothes to travel home in and I conceived the plan of going to Sears, where I could get everything I needed in one place: suitcase, underclothes, something cheap and sensible to wear—oh, how I hate to buy clothes for myself. William took me down and we wandered from department to department—he patiently following—examining the awful ragged-seamed suitcases, the clumsily made fake-leather shoes, the polyester and rayon dresses, the stretch jeans, the double-knit slack suits. I could not buy anything. He kept looking at me.

My children seem nowadays to look at me with kindness and pity in their eyes—I'm never quite sure why. My mortality affects them, perhaps.

He knew I was ready to weep, that tears were forming in my eyes.

"What's the matter?"

"You know how hard it is for me to make up my mind about clothes," I said. "And everything is so . . . I don't think I can buy anything."

We went back to his charred house and I flew across the country wearing a pair of his old khaki pants and a borrowed T-shirt, smelling like burnt toast.

But I started out to write down something else. One day, some two and a half years ago, I was trying to decide whether or not to buy a dress, had brought it home to show George. I put it on and came out into the living room and turned around for him. "What do you think? How does it look?"

He glanced at me and an expression of absolute revulsion and loathing blasted the air between us. "I don't know," he said, looking down again at his book. "It looks OK. Get it if you want it."

After that day I did not ask his opinion about my clothes. In fact, I stopped buying clothes altogether. Also, I dressed and undressed where he could not see me. He seemed unaware of the change in me.

In the fall when the last vacationing children and guests had departed and there was a free bed in the house, I left the bed we'd lain in back to back all those months, and moved to another room.

"Why are you moving?" he said.

"I can't sleep," I said. "You snore."

Both true. But the first was not the result of the second.

Later

So it wasn't at all that he was impotent. He was impotent with me. He didn't just not feel even the mildest interest in me, he was repelled by, he loathed me.

And perhaps he hardly knew it.

Not unusual after thirty years of marriage?

What difference does it make how common it is? What happens to other people doesn't make one's own anguish less sharp.

Still I waited. Things had changed before, hadn't they? He wouldn't go the rest of his life without sex, would he? There had, after all, been times when I had loathed him.

Sometimes I say to myself that he is so blindly obsessive, once he grabs something, he simply strides ahead, carrying it, gazing at it, absorbing it, forgets everything and everybody else. It was his absorption that made what happened next so immediately apparent to me. Not that he wanted it to be. Obviously, since, as it turned out, he didn't want a divorce—he was still fond of me, although he loathed me—and neither did she, it was to everyone's advantage to keep the affair under wraps. But he strode blindly ahead, holding his dream of her in his two hands, as it were. Even when I was in the room with them, he couldn't stop looking at her or thinking of her long enough to dissemble.

I watched them with a kind of vague, half-smug, half-anguished, half-enraged, half-excited sickness. At last something was going to happen. And, yes, there were more than enough pieces of me swelling with sick excitement inside one skin to make four or six or eight halves.

He'd never looked at another woman. I'd never felt even a twinge of jealousy. I'd said of him to my friends: He's the impossible, you know, a truly monogamous man.

Now he gazed at her and his face lit up. His voice caressed her. When she came into the room, it was as if somebody turned on a light in his head.

And she came, often enough, sweet as cream—at first, ostensibly, to see me, or both of us.

Here's how it went. They were people we knew—fifteen years younger, but they went to the same parties we went to. We saw them at concerts, at the movies, at the grocery store.

Four years ago they bought and remodeled an old house across the street from us, and before long we were visiting back and forth, as you do in a small city, borrowing a cup of sugar, exchanging recipes, praising each other's day lilies.

And then I began to notice how his face lit up. He would suggest we invite them over for a drink. I could hear in his voice that unmistakable naked tenderness. Or he'd see her in the yard in the late afternoon and go out and cross the street to visit with her. One evening, when the husband was working late and she came over alone, he touched her.

Except in the practice of his profession, with a stethoscope, a knife, a scalpel in his hand, he never touches anyone but us: the children, the grandchildren, me.

Friday Aug. 8th

From the time he was thirteen he never considered marrying anyone but me—or so he said, and I believed him.

I'd known him all my life. We were third cousins, raised in the same town, friends from early adolescence—whenever one starts being friends with the opposite sex. Not sexual friends —or not so far as I was concerned. He may have been yearning, but he was never the kind who laid himself open to rejection

16

and would have been even more protective of himself at fourteen and fifteen than he was later.

Later

This morning I started to write about George, but now I want to put down something else.

At the grocery store yesterday I saw an old woman (seventy-five, maybe? eighty?) staggering down the aisle pushing her shopping cart. She had very curly short yellow hair—not blond, but the yellow that white hair gets to be if you don't wash it often and don't put bluing on it. Bile yellow. She was skinny inside a baggy cotton housedress, her mouth distorted by ill-fitting false teeth. I couldn't stop looking at her legs and arms, the muscles like roots under the wrinkled skin—you know the ropy legs and arms of Donatello's "Magdalen"? And everywhere those terrible plum-colored and ocher bruises that come when the skin gets thin and the capillaries so fragile they break if you brush, even ever so lightly, against a table edge, a door facing. On one arm, just above the elbow, was a hematoma, a black lump with blue and plum-colored and gray and yellow fields of blood spreading out from it under the skin.

Already, if I'm not careful, I get small bruises like that. It's my vision, my depth perception. I'm still nearsighted in my left eye, but I've gotten quite farsighted in my right eye and I don't know exactly where things are. My eyes don't seem to be in communication with each other. For example, it's hard for me to home in with the tweezers on a chin whisker.

Yes, daughters, granddaughters, lovely girls with smooth faces, downy faces, as you get older, you get those, too.

Sunday Aug. 17th

As you can see by the date, more than a week has passed. That old woman . . .

But I *will* go on.

At fifty-nine—or was it sixty?—for the second time in the years of our marriage I fell in love with my husband.

Is this true? We've been married for so long, I simply cannot remember how I felt in all the different segments of time we've spent together.

Yes, I fell in love, for the second time in my marriage, the fourth time in my life. I was in love from the time I was twenty-four until I was twenty-eight with a man who was married to someone else. That love affair is probably not a part of this record and he is dead. Remembering him, remembering, too, my childhood, I can refer being in love even farther back in time. For of course I was first in love with my mother. I used to watch my two-year-old grandson stand on his mother's foot, wrap his arms around her leg as she worked at the kitchen counter and gaze passionately up at her. "Mama! Mama!" He was in love.

The summer I was eleven I was sent to camp—spent two months away from my mother. Later, the sensation I had in my stomach whenever I parted from my lover and sent him back to his wife, the sensation I have in my stomach right now, thinking of George, wherever he is, whoever he is with, are one and the same. There is a knot at the bottom. Above it, radiating out to points on my ribs directly under my arms, are lines of pain. At the top, in my chest, is a heavy, flat stone. I keep having to take deep breaths to hold it up, to keep it from crushing my lungs.

Summer mornings, when I wake and turn my head and see him sleeping sprawled beside me in his shorts—yes, we are sleeping together again—I feel a physical pleasure just looking at this sixty-year-old man—the kind of delight one feels at watching a sleeping child. His arm and his hand, lying open and relaxed against the white sheet, are brown and muscular. He is a vegetable gardener, spends a great deal of time outdoors under the sun; and his body has scarcely begun to go. His belly is flat—at least, like mine, it's flat when he's lying down. He's

18

stocky and, although he's beginning to go bald and his chestnut hair is heavily streaked with gray, the hair on his legs is still thick and curly and blond against his dark skin. The sunlight slants through our bedroom window, across our bed, and the hairs on his legs glint as if they're sprinkled with mica. I roll over and rub the sole of my foot against his warm familiar instep; its curve fits under my foot, the curves of his back against my thighs and belly as neatly as Africa would fit against South America, if it weren't for the intervening ocean.

At night I watch his face when he doesn't know I'm looking at him. He's reading, maybe. In the evenings, when he's finished his journals, he often reads and memorizes poetry. Poetry is his refuge, I suppose.

Any fool would have admired his legs and his chestnut hair forty years ago, but his face, to my doting eye, has become truly beautiful only with age. The lips, sensitive and sorrowful, almost ascetic; the eyes, dark green under heavy dark brows thickly threaded with gray, looking doubtfully, ironically at me; the nose getting bigger, as old men's noses do, but to me intimately pleasing, a nose I've known in all its moods and sizes.

He *is* more beautiful now than he was as a young man. It's not just that I have fallen in love with him again. Perhaps— yes, certainly—it's that memorizing poetry and looking at, patching up mangled bodies have formed his character and his face.

But to return to his love affair with the lady who moved across the street.

Here's the most outrageous, the most humiliating thing about it. She's unattractive. A toad. Never mind that she's fifteen years younger than I am. She is so short she can walk under the dining-room table without bending her head. Slight exaggeration. Really, she's four-eleven. But she has the look of someone who barely missed being a midget—arms a trifle short, a short-legged waddle for a walk. And that's the least of it. What's far worse is the smarmy, horrifying, idiotic, doting smile, the way she opens her eyes wide (she does have expressive eyes), lips parted (good mouth, too), and gazes up at him as if he's the cleverest, most wonderful thing that ever came down the pike.

But how would I like it if she were beautiful and witty and charming? Would that be better?

Later

When Ariadne sent Theseus into the labyrinth, she gave him the magical ball of thread that Daedalus had given her. She tied the thread end to the lintel at the entrance of the labyrinth and then she laid the ball on the floor and set it rolling and told Theseus to follow it. The rolling ball would lead him inward to the secret chamber where the Minotaur lived.

Some stories relate that Theseus killed the Minotaur and left him there, took up the thread, and followed it back to Ariadne; others that he subdued and bound the monster and brought him out alive. But there are other stories, too. The Cretans said there was no Minotaur—only a general named Taurus, an enemy of Ariadne's father, whom Theseus killed. Afterwards Ariadne was given him as his reward. The Cypriots said that it was Ariadne's brother Deucalion whom Theseus defeated in battle in order to give the throne to Ariadne, whom he controlled through her passion for him.

And then what happened to Ariadne? In some stories, Theseus abandons her on Naxos, where she marries the god Dionysus, in others she dies in childbirth on the island of Cyprus or hangs herself.

This morning, looking at the thread of ink drawing out across the page, I thought of myself as Ariadne setting the ball rolling into the labyrinth. But why should I cast myself in the ancient female part of victim of men's plots and passions? There are modern writers—the first of these, I believe, was a woman—who say that Ariadne's face and name—Most Holy

—mask the face and name of the great goddess, whom men have always feared.

But God knows I'm no goddess and have no desire to be. I want only to try to tell the truth that must be hidden somewhere inside the labyrinth of my dreams and passions and memories. I find myself thinking, not of the magical ball of thread that Theseus followed, but of the green stone that my son handed me in the Senoi dreamwork dream. But surely a stone won't be any use in a labyrinth, will it? Besides, in the dream, I am the one who must carry the stone.

Monday Aug. 18th

Why am I writing this? Why? There are two or three sets of reasons I could call up—that I will call up finally for what they're worth, if I have the stamina to stay with the search. I'll start with what seems to me the strongest. But to do that I have to begin before George and I were born.

And now, my children, although up to this point I have been addressing, and perhaps will again address, the world, a friend, myself, George—now I am talking to you.

George's grandmother—your great-grandmother—killed herself.

Commonplace event?

Not so. Did you know that only one in ten women who try to kill themselves succeed, while more than half the men do?

And here's what else is different about this suicide. No one knows about it except George and me. Could that possibly be true? That only a grandson and a great-niece-in-law, born years after you were dead, would know that you orphaned your children, abandoned them—and consigned yourself to hell? I must have dreamed it.

If I didn't, who concealed it? Why was it concealed?

21

I don't think it did or does matter very much to George. He is never subjective, hates personal emotion, personal crisis, sometimes, it seems to me, transforms or turns back emotions just as they touch his skin, before they reach the vital organs —probably out of fear that their strength will destroy him. As if someone were shooting dumdum bullets at him from a forty-four magnum pistol and he had some magical screening device at the epidermis that caught and turned the bullet before it spread and blew his liver to shreds.

Poetry maybe? Can it be that he memorizes poems, as if he were constructing walls, and that they surround him, turn aside every blow—that the "tyger" in the poem stands guard against my tiger claws?

Anyhow, it seemed to me, when I told him she had killed herself, that he registered the fact, filed it under some poem or other (Berryman, maybe. I think he even said, " '. . . down the bluff/ into the terrible water . . .' " but I was intent on telling him of my discovery and paid no attention), filed it, then, and thought no more of it.

But to go back to his grandmother. Briefly, to set up the family connections, George's grandfather and my grandmother were brother and sister. Our mothers were first cousins and we, therefore, are third cousins—distant enough so that no one remarked on our marriage, but raised almost like brother and sister because we lived in the same town and our mothers were good friends.

Although she died so long ago, I feel as if I knew her—that formidable lady who blew her brains out or poisoned herself or jumped in the river. (We don't know how she did it—only that she did.) I see her now in the fading photographs on the dressing tables of her children—George's aunt and uncle and his mother—one as a young girl on horseback, right leg hooked securely over the pommel of a sidesaddle, riding skirt sweeping down, bowler hat at a rakish angle; another the wedding photo-graph of a maiden in the elaborate sacrificial costume of the Victorian virgin, veiled and draped in lace and peau de soie.

And I hear my own grandmother's voice: "She could drive a six-foot wagon through a five-foot gate."

She had four children in a hurry during the eighteen eighties or nineties, lived, as so many Southern women did, on an isolated plantation, surrounded by black servants and black laborers. Her husband died of a burst appendix at thirty-five and she ran the farm single-handed.

"Ah, she was a wonder," my grandmother would say. "A real heroine. Nothing was too much for her."

She died when George's mother was sixteen, left her, the eldest daughter, the responsibility of her fourteen- and thirteen- and eleven-year-old siblings. They moved in with an uncle and his wife, but the younger ones always said that George's mother "raised" them. There was an older half-brother, but he was working in New Orleans, barely able to keep his own head above water.

How assiduously the family kept her memory alive—the intrepid horsewoman, the lovely bride, the courageous widow. They spoke of how little she cared for food; how not even the barrels of fresh oysters brought up from New Orleans—or Mobile or Galveston—or the Edam cheeses brought back from Memphis—or Atlanta or St. Louis—tempted her appetite. They always evoked her riding "as if she was born in the saddle" in her dashing habit, with the pale skin and fragile unearthly beauty of a Poe heroine, but the strong hands and arms of a horsewoman, the exuberance of a country girl. She would hitch herself to the goat cart and give the children, the babies, a ride around the front yard, lie down on the floor in front of the fire and romp with them. Father and mother both.

Ah, she was lovely, ah, everyone adored her!

And then the sad part. Three years of floods. The grueling grind of managing a failing plantation. Difficulties with banks, with labor, with boll weevils, with taxes. They lost the place.

"She worked herself to death . . ." So the story always ended.

"But what did she die of?" I remember asking as a child. They weren't sure. "A heart attack," one would say. "A stroke," another. Or, "We're not sure. You know how medicine was in those days . . . Unless you died of smallpox or something like that."

"But they knew what he died of."

"They operated on him, but it was too late."

Not just beauty—resourcefulness, joie de vivre, family feeling—all had their models in her.

During the summer six or seven years ago I took a part-time job at the Methodist church cataloguing, repairing, and restoring old records. (I like repetitive, mindless labor and I'd taken a course in records preservation at the college.) I was patching and mildew-proofing an old roll book when I came across her name—Rebecca Adams—and the dates of her birth and death. Beside the date of death, scrawled in another hand, was the word *Suicide*.

I looked again.

Suicide? *Suicide?*

The parish house floor, the continental shelf, tilted slightly under my feet. I read the word and the name again. Was there another Rebecca Adams in that generation, a cousin, perhaps? Or even someone unconnected? Adams, after all, is a not uncommon name. I wrote down the dates, closed the ledger, locked the parish house, got into my car, drove directly to the cemetery, to the lot, and went straight to her grave. I looked at her stone. The dates were the same. I went home.

I must, it appeared, believe one of the following:

A. My great-aunt-in-law, George's grandmother, did in fact kill herself. This was known to the whole community of my older relatives and friends—my parents, George's parents, our aunts, uncles, and cousins, and all their friends and acquaintances; and by some impossibly rigid, unbreakable agreement among them all—scores, hundreds of people—they concealed it from George and me.

B. George's mother knew it and her older brother and perhaps a small number of other people—the doctor? the undertaker? the preacher?—but they conspired to conceal it from their younger siblings, from their own children, and eventually from us. Nevertheless, someone, for some reason—the preacher, perhaps, in an access of honesty, afraid God might be mad at him for this deception—wrote that word in the church roll book.

C. Even George's mother did not know.

D. She did not kill herself at all. The word was meant to go by someone else's name.

There are other possibilities, but those are enough to begin with.

As soon as George got home from the hospital, I told him what I'd found. This was before he went into emergency-room medicine, but there had been two wrecks and he had been in surgery all night.

"I've got to get some sleep," he said. "Tell me tomorrow. I'm getting too old for all-night surgery."

"It's your doing," I said. "You could have called William Boswell in to relieve you." I was irritated because I was sure he wasn't all that tired—surgery exhilarates him—he was simply putting the screen in place.

When he'd slept eight hours and eaten a midafternoon breakfast and had a couple of cups of coffee, he listened to me as I outlined the possibilities. "Why did she do it?" I said. "Who could have written it?"

He shook his head judiciously and looked longingly at the morning paper, which he likes to read while he drinks his coffee.

My mother, all our aunts and uncles, were dead. "We could ask your mother," I said.

The absent-mindedness went out of his eyes. "Under no circumstances," he said. "Never!"

"No," I said. "Of course we can't." His mother was already past eighty, beginning to fix her stoic gaze on death. "But . . . But George, I feel as if everything in the world has changed. I feel dislocated. I don't know, after all, who anybody is, where we came from."

"What's the use in talking about it?" he said. "It happened before we were born and has nothing to do with us—if it happened at all."

"We're talking about your mother," I said. "About what formed her life. About her mother—her heroine."

" '. . . Well, we must labor and dream . . .' " He smiled at me half apologetically.

Berryman again.

"George!" I said.

"I'm off tomorrow," he said. "Would you like to go fishing?"

His mother died the following year, the last person who might have been able to tell us the truth.

I couldn't stop thinking about it. I kept sliding down that slightly tilting continental plate. Who could say whether I wouldn't slide right into the New Madrid Fault?

So that's why I began to think about writing things down, explaining things. She, that remote old great-aunt-in-law, dead seventy years, has changed my way of thinking about every relationship, every character, every person in our joint family. Nothing is what it seemed. The facts of my life, my history, their lives, on which I had a tenuous hold at best, dissolve like smoke before my face and vanish away. Why should I believe anything about them, about anyone, if I can't believe what they said about her, whom they loved so passionately, so assiduously kept alive?

And I would rather give you, my children, my grandchildren, something else. I would like you to know me (know George, too, but that's his business. I can't give you him, only my crazy version of him), so that you can know that part of yourselves that is me. At least I would like not to give you a gross pack of lies.

Until now, I know, we have always presented ourselves to you as parents, as people leading orderly and serene lives, who have been at great pains to teach you by example, decency, responsibility, et cetera, who perhaps appear to you, as parents do, removed from the doubt and anguish and questionable passion that torment real people.

But I am not serene, not orderly, not decent. No. None of these.

And there is no way to tell you, just talking, how and why . . . No matter how the conversation goes, it doesn't seem true when we have finished.

And, oh, I love you. I want to embrace and cherish you, to give you—*something*. My beautiful Corinne. I love the way you walk, tilted forward, abstracted, your lips set, hurrying to get everything done. And my judicious James, weighing, reserving judgment, making things work. And William, singing, singing. It's for you I try to understand, to you I write.

Later

Not to change the subject, but I want you to think of me as being like the best women in Joyce Cary's novels—the heroine of the Nimmo trilogy, for example. I want to present myself unselfconsciously, but in a way so that when you have read all I have to say, I will be known as marvelously vital, generous-hearted, courageous, and passionate (like your great-grandmother). But I will also be modest. I won't have dreamed of praising myself.

I'm digressing. The mystery of that old woman's death . . .

But she was not old, although I have always thought of her in her last picture, familiar to me since childhood, as ancient. In it she sits in the photographer's studio in an ornate mock-Renaissance chair with a high velvet back and twisted arms, in a matronly pose, one arm around the child leaning against her knee. Her dark hair is caught in a loose knot low on her neck; she wears a severe high-necked basque with an onyx pin at the throat, and on her lips is the sad, piercingly ironic smile that is so like George's. But that picture must have been made when she was in her middle thirties, young enough to be my child.

The mystery of her life then, her death, like a heavy shadow, obscures the passionate, vivid woman whom my grandmother and George's mother created for me: the devoted wife and mother, the gallant-hearted widow fighting for her farm, the horsewoman whom my mother recalled bending down to lift her up to the saddle for a ride.

Why did she abandon them? Why? And why did they lie?

That shadow, then, hangs over every word, my children, my darlings, that I write to you.

Tuesday Aug. 19th

I begin again. Here is a possible version of what happened to George and me and The Toad.

After that day when he touched her shoulder, I never had the least doubt what was going on. But now my attention was on something else. Knowing George, I knew that he would turn the bullet—would never admit to the affair; that he would simply tell me I was imagining things, maybe even tell me I must be getting senile. And then he would go his way, trying absent-mindedly to be more careful. Also, I said to myself, maybe you *are* senile—crazy. So I had two things to do. First I had to wait and watch and evaluate myself, to make sure I wasn't crazy. Second, in order to be absolutely certain I was not, I had to put him in a position where there would be no way he could deny what was happening. Then we'd see.

Was it at this point that I began to fall back in love with him? No, I think it must have been later. I did, however, begin to take a deeper interest in the events of our lives.

Poor George. What a curse my interest has turned out to be for him.

The way to make sure I wasn't crazy, I decided, was to catch him in a lie—in some kind of deceit. Because he always used to have a thing about lying. He would tell the truth when it would have been easier to lie, when it might even have been the decent thing to do. For example, trapped in church—say he's a pallbearer, sitting on the front row, across the aisle from the bereaved family—he stands through prayers with his head unbowed, his eyes open, keeps his lips closed when everyone else is reciting the Lord's Prayer. That's not honesty—that's mulishness, intellectual pride.

But, because of his pride, I knew that there was no way he would lie unless it was vital to him.

Catching him turned out to be more than easy. He caught himself, with scarcely a lifted finger from me. All I did was come home from the college in the middle of the afternoon one day—considerably earlier than he was expecting me—to find the dog on the chain outside the front door. (When I turn in at the driveway, the dog barks at me as if I am a jewel thief, an ax murderer.) Having been alerted by faithful Fideau, they —G. and The Toad—were sitting, by the time I got in the house, in the living room, decorous as two ladies having afternoon tea together. But her face was flushed and he looked simple-minded with anxiety—jumped around, smiling and nodding at me as if I were a visitor from another planet. Later I observed that the bed I'd left straight was rumpled.

Still, that occasion was only a first step. It wasn't enough, I knew—not a real lie, only suspicious behavior. I couldn't confront him with anything as innocuous as that occasion appeared to be—perhaps was.

It was still not possible to be sure I was sane.

What to do to be absolutely sure? Patience was everything. I had to let them make their bed (ha ha!) and lie in it.

I had a great-aunt who spent the last ten years of her life believing she was a prisoner in a whorehouse. My darlings, that's not funny, either, although it sounds as if it should be. It would have been fine if she had been happy—a volunteer and successful—but she wasn't.

During those weeks, when I was away from home, at work, or when I was sure G. was with her, I went through the motions of my life as if I were asleep. Obsessively I was with them— as if I were the spirit in their dreams, or they in mine.

Oh, it's all so strange. Why was I excited? Why, when we had not made love for almost a year, when I was sixty years old, when the time had come for some sort of tolerant friendship between us, when the fire in the labia should be dying, did George's affair have such an effect on me? And not, to be precise, the effect of causing me unadulterated grief. The effect, rather, of an agonizing, but at the same time, glorious excitement. After thirty years, could it be that I believed we would at last get acquainted? That I could force him to reveal himself to me? Could blast our life together out of that awful groove that thirty-year-old marriages grate along? That some magical revelation would come, some whole transformation of our lives, when I told him I knew he was screwing The Toad?

Yes. That, indeed, is what I thought would happen. Not with my head, but with some yearning, anguished part of me. I would confront him, embrace him. I would forgive. He would regret. Deep understanding would follow. Our love would grow stronger.

He would desire me.

I continued patient, crazy. More weeks passed. I lost ten pounds I could ill afford to lose.

They handed me the next occasion on a silver platter. I didn't have to set it up. By chance, on a Thursday afternoon, I saw his car in an extraordinary place.

He was supposed to be on duty at the hospital—had driven off after lunch in that direction. I left almost immediately afterwards and took a pile of blankets, bed linens, and discarded clothes down to the Salvation Army, from which an emergency call had gone out the day before for a burned-out family. On my way home, driving through a middle-class neighborhood in the process of disintegrating into a slum, I saw his car.

What? What's he doing?

Before my obsessive eye The Toad instantly appeared. I drove on two blocks, turned left, circled past his car, and cast again in the opposite direction.

Of course.

There was her car, a block from his in the parking lot at the side of a little mission church in which, as I very well knew, since she had talked boringly about it on more than one occasion, she took an interest.

Now, The Toad is very churchy. She cares passionately about arranging the altar flowers and polishing the communion brass. (Is the communion service brass? Except to restore those roll books, I haven't been to church voluntarily since I was fifteen, an ignorant on these subjects. I go to funerals and occasionally to the wedding of a friend's child and that's it. Not that I don't care desperately about God and all that, but that church . . . It's—I don't know—crazy, useless, boring. I don't know what to make of it. George is even less churchy than I, but he always listened with a tender smile to The Toad's parish gossip—even advised her about a couple of her projects.)

Anyhow, the church where her car was parked—a little knocked-together building sheathed in asbestos shingles with a skinny prefab steeple on top and an ell to one side for the Sunday School—is a mission supported by The Toad's more affluent downtown First Methodist; and I knew that she was a kind of sponsor and liaison person between the two and that her husband, who was equally churchy, was sometimes a lay preacher there.

"I wish you'd come hear him sometime," she said to us once. "He'd bring you straight to Jesus."

George hadn't even the grace to look embarrassed.

But to go back to this Thursday afternoon.

My heart was leaping against my ribs like Fideau against his chain when a Doberman pinscher urinates on his favorite tree. My eyeballs felt as if I'd been struck by an acute attack of glaucoma, my ears thundered and stung as if moths might be fluttering inside, an ant biting my eardrum.

What in the world?

I circled the block again, parked my car on the opposite side of the church from hers, where it would not be visible if they came out, and walked around the corner of the building toward the side door nearest her car.

I was not thinking. I didn't know what I meant to do. Was I awake or dreaming? By the time I got to the door I had changed my mind about concealing myself. I would go in and announce myself.

"Toad, darling! I saw your car and you've talked so much about your mission. I wanted to see it. What a darling sanctuary." Et cetera, et cetera. "Yes, George and I are both so interested in it, aren't we, George?" I didn't care how lame it sounded. I was crazy.

The door was open and I pushed it in as silently as I could. Already I had changed my mind again. I would avoid them, eavesdrop on them, find out some truth that I could not learn if I confronted them. The moths kept thundering in my ears.

Let me say here that I used to be a reasonably decent person. I have never opened anyone's personal letter. I did not eavesdrop on your adolescent telephone conversations, children. I knocked, did I not, at your doors before entering? I did not cheat on exams—or only once and that occasion still haunts me; or steal trinkets from the dime store for kicks—or, if I did, I do not remember it. But of course none of these temptations has to do with sex.

So I went into the church.

I am inside. Ahead of me, a hall with three closed doors on either side. These must be the Sunday School rooms and church offices. From beyond a half-open door at the far end of the hall I hear the murmur of voices. Theirs?

Silently I open the first door on the left. It's the nursery. Half a dozen cribs and as many cots. A couple of chairs. Across the hall, behind another door, the preacher's study. I hear echoing footsteps in what must be the sanctuary. Coming toward me? The moths are interfering.

Hastily I open the next door on the left, step inside, close it, and look around. Are they coming here? Probably not. This must be the church play school. Blocks and toys and coloring books stacked on low shelves around the room, small chairs and long low tables in the center of the room. The footsteps and voices are getting louder.

What an ass I am! An ass! The moths thunder. I see them

33

against the panes of a row of uncurtained windows—clothes moths, their wings a blur of gray, jumping black spots like frightened crickets, crawling rows of dots. Ants? Something seems to brush against my face. I feel as if I might be drawing insects into my lungs with every breath.

A door.

I stumbled across the room, opened it, stepped into a closet, and faced another door. The closet opened into both rooms. Shelves on one side stacked with small pillows and bed linens, worn cotton blankets, grayish often-mended sheets, on the other with plastic plates, cutlery, glasses. I drew the door closed behind me, leaving it cracked. I couldn't bear to close it all the way—the dark! The airless dark! I slid—huddled—to the floor, drew my legs close to my chest, put my head on my knees.

Oh, why am I here? Why am I suffering? A blanket, gray in the closed-in half-light, lay on the floor beside me. I picked it up and began to examine it, selvedge by selvedge, patch by patch. I made out the tag attached to one corner: Crib size: 54″ × 60″. I crushed it against my face, breathed in the clean cottony smell of childhood, could not weep for fear I might be heard.

I heard them enter the room next door, the nursery. Sitting on the floor, close to the door that opened on their side, I could hear their voices clearly, understand everything they said. As soon as she spoke, the moths sat still in my head. Not another flutter.

"Well?" She giggled. Tittered!

I heard a scraping noise, the sound of springs creaking.

"Pull the mattress off and put it on the floor," she said.

"I just wanted to see you. To hold you for a few minutes. To talk." (George.)

Silence. Thirty seconds? I closed my eyes and began to count, as if I were taking my temperature: one, Mississippi, two, Louisiana, three Tennessee.

"I want you," she said in that hoarse, passionate, toadish voice, too heavy for her slight body.

34

Where is Jesus? Is He holding her hand?

More silence. Presumably they're embracing.

"I don't like it," he said. "For you. We can be more re-sourceful than this."

Oh, I shouldn't be writing this. She's not "churchy." She cares about her little church. About Jesus. But George? Does she care about George? Do I? And me? Does anyone care about me?

Then, "You know I don't want to get you into a messy situation," he said.

Silence.

"Last weekend . . . The water . . . The moonlight . . ."

Moonlight? George?

He'd told me he had a twenty-four-hour shift at the hospital Friday.

"Yes, that's how it ought to be," she said, "but it isn't always possible."

Silence again.

"Listen, George. No one *ever* comes here on Thursday after-noons. And suppose someone did come? We can lock the nursery door. It's OK. All right? They would think nothing of it's being locked. In this neighborhood doors are usually locked —inside doors as well as outside ones. But no one ever comes here on Thursday afternoon. Mornings, yes. Wednesday for choir practice, yes. Friday and Saturday, sometimes. But not Thursday afternoon."

Silence. Muffled shiftings and movements.

"I won't put you through this again," he said.

"I'd better go lock the outside door."

I heard the door open, crushed the blanket against my breast. What am I doing here? It's time to leave. Footsteps. The door closed and the latch clicked.

"You didn't waste any time," she said. Giggled.

Is he naked?

I get up. Enough. I'm leaving. I step out of the closet, tiptoe across the room, slowly ease open the door into the hall, step out. Forty feet away, from beyond the door she just locked, I hear voices. Good God, now what? I return to my closet.

From the hall, women's voices. Laughter. In the next room, silence.

"Shh . . ."

"For God's sake, somebody's coming in."

After this one sentence, the silence in the next room is unbroken. I am listening with one ear for them, with the other to the voices in the hall. I imagine what George and The Toad are doing. G. is pulling on his slacks, buttoning his shirt. Shoes? Maybe he hasn't taken them off—they were in such a fucking hurry. Now they are staring, wordlessly, frantically at each other. He straightens her collar.

Then, from the room on the far side of mine, I hear piano chords, a female voice, contralto, limbering up with scales. The piano goes into, "Draw me nearer, nearer, nearer, blessed Lord . . ."

I find that I am giggling, smothering my head in the blanket.

"They can't possibly hear us in here." (The Toad again.) "They're two doors down, in the choir room." Then: "Relax," she says. "They're not coming in here. They can't. I have the key. Remember? OK?"

In a moment he laughs. That deep quiet chuckle. "Jesus Christ, you're crazy, you know it? You're a kid. You make me feel like a kid."

"Just be quiet," she says. "OK?"

Silence.

"Ahhhh . . ."

"Shh . . ."

On the other side, the piano trails the sour contralto into another number. " 'Just as I a-am, without one plea/ Just as I a-am, I come to Thee . . .' "

"Aren't you ashamed?" he says, laughing still, and then, moaning, "Oh, yes . . ."

" 'Just as I a-am and waiting not . . .' "

"Jesus!" he says. He often says *Jesus* when he comes.

I'm tired. I don't care any more whether anyone sees me or not. I cross the room, open the door, making no effort to be quiet, walk down the echoing hall . . .

" 'Just as I a-am, Thy love I own . . .' "

Ugh. Flat.

I unlock the outside door, which the choir ladies have latched behind them, leave the church, go to my car, and get in. I sit a few minutes. The street is empty. I get out of the car, and keeping the door open, face inward, bend down to shield myself from anyone who may be looking out the window of a nearby house, and vomit. I stare at the hinge of the car door for a few minutes. Then I get back in and sit with my hands on the wheel. The tears that are forced by vomiting are on my cheeks. I find a Kleenex in my purse and wipe them away. From here I can see a row of windows along the ell of the church. As I sit looking, George climbs out of one and walks unhurriedly away toward his car. His back is toward me, and anyhow I am across the street and half a block away.

I watch him walk—the dear, familiar, slightly slew-footed walk, the erect almost swayback carriage. Is he reciting a poem to himself? Blake, maybe? " 'The lust of the goat is the glory of God . . .' "

My ears. Moths? Ants? I start the car and drive away. On the car radio Dolly Parton is singing.

I turned the radio off and drove slowly, in silence, around the town where we live, up one street and down another, filled with a curious empty sick exultation and anguish. Does he want a divorce? Shall I tell him what I know? How can I tell him without telling the humiliating truth that I have spied on him? You see, I said to myself, you were right, you knew in your bones that this craziness would break the ice block we've been embedded in all these months. But now? Now what?

Ah, illusions. Pitiful sad illusions.

I took the ramp up onto the bypass, drove south a few miles, and took the False River exit onto a straight stretch of two-lane blacktop road ending at the lake. I put the accelerator on the floor and drove ten miles as fast as I could. I am a good driver and this is a good car. The road was empty. Then I turned around and drove back to town. It was five o'clock. George would come home around eleven, tired. I stopped at the liquor store and picked up a fifth of bourbon.

Probably I won't have a drink, I said to myself. I want one, true, but I need to keep a clear head. I'll listen to the five-thirty news.

Then what?

Thursday Aug. 28th

Shall I tell you, children, about our courtship? I've always shied away from such talk with you. I wrote last week—and afterwards came close to deciding to write no more, but after all, here I am again—anyhow, I wrote, "He never considered marrying anyone but me," etc., but then I got sidetracked. I put off saying how things were between us. I suppose the reason I never talked to you about our courtship was that in a way it put us both in a less than heroic, less than romantic light and, mysteriously, one wants one's children to have romantic and heroic illusions about courtship. Besides, of course, court-ships are private. You haven't told me much about yours and I haven't asked you.

But now privacy is what I want to throw away, to get rid of. How can one value privacy over truth?

"Wait!"

Now who's speaking? I hear in my head, as if I were half asleep, inviting the Senoi dream state, a question, spoken with my own private voice, a voice without substance, without reso-nance, known to no one but me.

"Truth?" she says. "So you think you can borrow George's scalpel and set about methodically, like the maniacal doctor in *The Bride of Frankenstein,* flaying yourself alive? Do you re-member that scene? The shadow of the agonized figure shrink-ing from the shadow of the doctor with his knife?

"Then what will you do? Will you stuff the skin with hay? There's a bale left over from mulching the asparagus bed. Will you paint the lips and eyelids and fingernails green, hang it by its hair in a glass case? And the bloody carcass? What will you do with that? And which is you—the skin or the meat?"

39

I remain calm. "Have you a gift for me?" I say. I am sitting at my desk with my eyes open, the morning sun slanting in at my window. I do not hear her, but rather see her words in my head and see there, too, a scene, as if from a movie. A vague tall figure raises the knife, breaks the glass case, jerks down and drags out the stuffed dummy, and shoves it at me; picks up the bloody shredded body from the floor and drapes it over my shoulder. "Here!"

"That's no gift," I say. "I've already got these. I'm trying to get rid of them."

The facts are these: It's true that he was "always in love with me, never looked at another woman." The kind of obsessive love that begins when you are thirteen and never wavers. She —he—is all you want.

But I was two years older, and besides, he was my cousin. I paid no attention to how he felt—too busy with my own feelings. Or I pretended not to notice—to spare him the humiliation of knowing that I recognized his unrequited passion, as well as to spare myself inconvenience.

We rode and fished together all through high school and college, because riding and fishing were what we liked to do. I treated him like a brother, he told me I should kiss my elbow and turn into a boy. I halfway agreed. Later I told him about my romances, my "crushes," and he listened and rejoiced or comforted me, as the occasion demanded.

And he had his romances—one or two lukewarm ones. Later . . . I don't know what went on for him during the war years. He would never say—or said, rather, that it didn't matter.

Let's see, let me try to get the chronology of our lives straight.

1918—I am born.

1920—George is born.

1934—George falls in love with me. I am sixteen, he is fourteen.

1939—I graduate from college. George is just a year behind me. He's doubled up on courses because he's bright and wants to go into medical school as early as he can. And he does, in the fall of 1940, after graduating from college in three years.

1941—Pearl Harbor, of course. George finishes his second year of med school and could go on, as they're not drafting medical students; but in an access of patriotism, in June of 1942, he quits and joins the army.

1942—I am teaching in the city of my birth, also working on my M.A. (We have a middling good small Methodist college, and I have taught in it off and on for twenty-five years.) I fall in love with a man twenty years older than I, a man with a wife and several children, and begin an affair with him.

1945—I am twenty-seven, still in love with the married man, still taking crumbs from that table. George goes back to med school as soon as he gets out of the service.

1946—My lover dies. I go to George for comfort, as I have many times in the past, but now in a more thoroughgoing way.

God knows what, if anything, was in my mind. I felt I had to leave the town I'd yearned in for the past four years, the town that held on every corner, under every tree some memory of his beloved voice, some glimpse of his figure walking away from me, the streets where now his sons (not mine) were growing up.

Where to go? I went to the city where George was finishing med school, getting ready to do his internship, and got a job there. I could talk to him and, in fact, to no one else about my great tragedy. I would go where he was.

What happened next—and again, I scarcely know why or how—was that within six months I married him. I was twenty-nine. I was exhausted. I loved him like a brother. I wanted, needed a refuge. He wanted me. I committed myself to him, to his life.

When I say I loved him like a brother, I don't mean to imply that I did not intend to have sex with him, that I entered the marriage with any such serious reservation as that. Not at all. Of course I expected it to be a sexual relationship. I expected us to raise a family—marriage without children was inconceivable to me and I'm sure my age—the childbearing years rushing away—must have been one of the reasons I hurried into the marriage. But it was to be a marriage in which the old friendship was the iron link and the sexual relationship not particularly important. I'd had enough—only for the moment, as it turned out—of my own sexual obsessions.

And then? Then I fell in love with him.

Four or five times in one's life, I suppose, one has this kind of experience, wakes up a new person. I looked at him one day and . . .

It was six months into his internship. He was working extra shifts in the emergency room to pick up cash, and I was teaching and working on my Ph.D. Interns were ill-paid in those days (teachers, too, of course) and we had to scramble to make ends meet.

He'd lost a patient. I could say I remember who it was: a beautiful and brilliant young girl, a courageous child—someone who brought home to him in a poignant way the bitter tragedy of human fate; but I don't remember. He's lost so many patients; there have been so many days when he's looked like that.

He came in and sat down in our tiny living room in our little box house and filled it with his grief.

I looked at him, his hair, still damp with sweat, plastered down like a child's against his scalp, his closed, worn young face.

I love him, I said to myself. I love him. My heart, my liver swelled up like the bubble in the throat of a courting frog. The years of anguish and yearning, for a man I could never have, split open like the rigid chrysalis of a seventeen-year locust and I crawled out and unfolded a new set of wings—looked back at the hollow shell of my old self, clinging like a creature from outer space, a monster, to the barky fiber of our cheap plaited straw living-room rug. I flew away into a new life.

I went to the couch and sat down and put my arms around him. I wanted him to lay his head against my breast, wanted to take his pain to myself, to free him from it; but I dared not tell him how I felt, for he would then know how much more than he realized I had not felt before. I had, of course, made all the motions that the honeymoon required, acted out a passion deeper than I had been capable of.

He shook his head stiffly, holding it a little to one side, away from me, as if he might have a crick in his neck, gently moved my arms, and stood up. "I'll be OK," he said. He went into the bedroom and closed the door behind him.

So, as it turned out, my loving him like that was never much use to him and was a torment to me. I thought we would move now deeper into the passionate carnal friendship of true marriage, that this would happen because *I* loved *him*—because, instead of wanting to tell him about my feelings, explore and come to terms with my past, I wanted to know more, more, more about him. But he had been in the habit since childhood of concealing from me, not only his humiliating adolescent passion for me but, as time passed, the pain that my long futile affair gave him, concealing everything except his willingness to support and cherish me.

It may be that to begin with he fell in love with me because he needed to conceal himself—that he chose me because I didn't love him, wouldn't put my attention on him. Could that be?

And I? What about me?

Friday Aug. 29th

That night—the night of The Toad and the church—he came home not long after ten o'clock. Again he'd been taking part of a shift for an absent intern. It had been an easy day, he said. No real crises.

I had been thinking.

43

Better, to begin with, to tell him what I knew, find out what he intended, what he wanted. Did he want a divorce? Did she? But how could I tell him without putting myself in a humiliating light, presenting myself as gross, despicable, a sneak, a spy? I couldn't bear to do that—I had to hang on to some shred of dignity. And what about him? I had to save his pride, too. Could I say I'd seen him climbing out the church window? *George?* At his age? No!

I'm sitting in my usual chair, he's sitting in his, a book in his hand. Reading Berryman again? Yes, it's *The Dream Songs*.

A drink for me? No, I want a clear head. Coffee. Yes, coffee's the thing. What does it matter whether it keeps me awake or not if it keeps me calm now? I go to the kitchen and fix a pot, pour myself a cup, and return to my place in the living room.

"George?"

He looked up.

I think it must be that I always make a pot of coffee and sit down with a particular look on my face when I want to talk about something important—because he didn't respond, as he might under other circumstances, with an absent-minded "Hmmm?" He looked up, laid down his book, and said, "Yes?"

"I have something I want—   There's something we need to talk about."

He folded his arms across his chest, drew in a sprawled foot. "All right. What?"

My heart was pounding, my hand holding the coffee cup trembling. I set the cup on the table. "I know," I said. The moths thundered in my ears, but I went on: "I know you are —are involved with . . ." I called her name. "I've known it for awhile."

"What? I'm what?"

"I suppose I've known it ever since I saw you put your hand on her shoulder," I said. "Maybe even before that. You never touch anyone but us. Never."

"What's gotten into you?" he said. His face was as expressionless as it must be when he's cutting a fishhook out of a

44

child's finger. "What's wrong with you? I'm not—*involved*—with anyone."

"—and then, the day Fideau was on his chain . . ." I said.

"Fido!" He spells it one way, I spell it the other. He began to shake his head slowly.

"Let me finish," I said. And I went on through the song and dance I'd thought up and rehearsed while I waited for him, about thirty-year-old marriages and the inevitability of affairs, how I understood. This was a chance for magnanimity.

"I love you," I said. "I trust you. We can survive it."

"Trust me!" He shrugged. "The fact of the matter is that I haven't the least interest in an affair with anyone," he said.

"Oh, George," I said. "I know."

"Of course I like her," he said reasonably. "We're friends. I thought you liked her, too. I thought we liked them both. He's . . ." He was hard put to it to say what "he" was, since at best he's a dull tool. "She's lively. We have a lot in common. Gardening . . . But an affair? Don't be ridiculous, Corinne. You know me better than that, don't you?"

"No," I said. "I don't know you at all."

He sat looking at me, waiting, his face closed, the green eyes remote.

"I called you at the emergency room last Friday night," I said. "They said you weren't on duty—weren't there. Where were you?" Friday was the moonlit night they'd mentioned.

That stopped him for only a fraction of a second.

"I don't know who told you that," he said. "Of course I was on duty. I spent a couple of hours up on third with Frank Carroll. I told you he'd had a strangulated hernia, didn't I?"

"Yes," I said. Since I was lying—I hadn't called Friday night at all—I couldn't press him. Maybe he did take part of the shift to visit Frank. "You weren't there when I called," I said again.

"Do you want me to bring you an affidavit from Mrs. Lamb?" She's the emergency nurse on the night shift.

How safe he must have felt! Why? Because of his obsessiveness, his absorption. Everything, everyone must give way to make room for his passion.

"Oh, George, be cautious. Be careful. We have to find some way to reach each other. Do you want a divorce? Does she?"

"A divorce! Of course I don't want a divorce. Are you crazy?"

"George," I said, "where were you today?"

"As a matter of fact I left the hospital for a couple of hours and went out to Sears for . . ."

"I saw your car," I said.

"At Sears?"

"No. I saw your car parked over on South Broad."

Oh, oh, oh. This is all wrong, all wrong.

Later

I can't, after all, make up a true lie. That's what I thought of my story of The Toad as being—a *true lie*. A waking dream that would bring its gift of meaning to us all. I would use it to tell about our crisis, our distress. I would save his privacy. My . . .

My what? A few shreds of my pride? But is this lie, after all, one that presents me in a good light?

And then, what did I intend to do after I had finished slandering The Toad?

I don't know. I don't know. I didn't think. I can't think.

Later

When I was eight or nine and my older brother was eleven, we sneaked off one Saturday afternoon to see Lon Chaney in *The Unholy Three*. Remember that old movie? Lon Chaney played the part of a dwarf in it. (Just a coincidence. No connection with The Toad.) A gang of thieves used him to climb through openings too small for normal adults and to open doors to them for their robberies.

46

My mother had forbidden us to see it. Perhaps it was that word "unholy." She was a devout Methodist. It's possible *The Bride of Frankenstein* was made respectable enough for us to see by the word "bride" in the title, even though there was a monster in it. But no unholy movies for her children. Or perhaps she thought with good reason that we were too suggestible to be permitted to see Lon Chaney movies. Whatever her reason, she had forbidden us to go to it.

Afterwards my brother went his way without a thought, but I was consumed by guilt. I thought not at all of Lon Chaney and his horrible colleagues and his pitiful, suffering, evil face, only of my own disobedience.

Why was I cursed with this guilt, while my brother was free of it? Evidently my parents had not laid such a burden on him, or, if they had, he had refused it. He was merry as a chirping cricket.

And what was happening in my twisted childish soul? I seem to hear my mother's voice—and my own, later, saying the same thing to you, children: *The truth! We can't depend on each other unless we tell each other the truth.*

God alone knows why I thought that movie was the ultimate test of my honor. Surely I have forgotten other occasions when for some reason confession seemed unnecessary—just as God alone knows what's going on with me now (Oh, whatever happens, I commit myself to the truth, etc., etc., in the midst of this thicket of lies.)

In any case, I went to my brother and told him that I could not keep our guilty secret another day. And, ergo, I had to tell on both of us. It occurs to me now that I didn't have to tell her I went with him—I could have left him out of it. But he didn't suggest that. He just said, "Go on and tell, *baby*. I don't care."

So I did, expecting punishment, expiation, relief, purity. But my mother said, only, "Well, it doesn't seem to have hurt either of you, does it? You haven't been having nightmares or anything like that, have you?"

"No," I said.

"Well, don't worry about it, then."

Now listen: Neither my mother nor my brother recalled this episode in our lives when, reminiscing one day, I asked them about it.

But I know it happened. I remember the room where Mama was sitting when I told her, the time of the summer afternoon, four o'clock sunlight slanting through the shuttered windows, the smell of cut grass, the drowsy tick of the old reel mower blades turning.

Even though I understand at least some of the significance of this story, I can't stop to think about it, to analyze it. I have to go on, just as I did then.

Why? Why did she kill herself—if she did?

Why did they conceal it?

Here are some possibilities, bizarre and less bizarre, that I have considered.

A. Remember the isolated rural world she lived in, her widowed state, her loneliness. Sometimes, perhaps, an aunt, a sister, a cousin would come and stay for weeks; sometimes, particularly during the winter months, she would bring the children to town. And in the planting season, surely neighboring planters would pass by on their way to town from their own isolated farms, would stop in to advise her, would stay for lunch or for the night. But she was alone, the only white adult on the farm for weeks, even months at a time. She was a young woman, in her sexual prime. It happened, therefore, not surprisingly, that she got involved sexually with an unsuitable man (an overseer, maybe, or a married man who lived on a neighboring farm? A Negro!), a man she couldn't or didn't want to marry; she got pregnant . . . But surely she could have found someone to abort her, couldn't she? Maybe she loved him to distraction, couldn't live without him . . .

B. She discovered that she had a painful and fatal disease.

C. She became addicted to alcohol or drugs (not uncommon in those days before people knew much about the addictive effects of morphine) and decided the children would be better off without her.

Why did they conceal it? And how? The why is perhaps answerable. The how is another matter.

They concealed it because:

A. They didn't want the children to know their mother had abandoned them, or

B. Suicides and bastard offspring were non-happenings and non-persons among such pious and respectable people.

Do you know the story of the love affair between the parents of John Dos Passos? She was an upper-middle-class Southern widow and he was a successful—and married—Detroit lawyer. He moved her and their illegitimate son from city to city, from country to country. They lived in obscure hotels and he visited them in secret. His wife, he claimed, would not divorce him. In those days it was women and children last in some lifeboats.

Somehow, none of my explanations seems valid to me. Perhaps because she—George's grandmother—was presented to us as courageous, as forceful; because they, the family, presented themselves as honest, as earnestly enjoining honesty.

No, there was never the faintest shadow in a single face bending down to me in my childhood, never a shrugged shoulder, a raised eyebrow, a quirky smile that said, "Ah, but you see how it is. We're not what we seem. It can't be helped."

Saturday Sept. 6th

Registration was Monday and Tuesday of this week and now the semester has begun. I am teaching six hours and have no classes before ten o'clock—privilege of seniority.

I don't intend to let work become another device for postponing.

And this time I'll try to be straight with you.

I've at least been straight enough thus far to say obliquely that another major reason for writing this down is to justify myself—to you, children, and to myself, perhaps to the world. Remember what I said about Joyce Cary's heroines?

I suppose—Corinne, William, James—that all of you, though you won't say it, are thinking: Well, Mama, after all, credit us with a little sense. We're not simple-minded. We know that nobody has entirely untainted motives.

To begin with, then, it was not The Toad. Not at all. It was someone else.

What difference does it make, you may ask, whether you choose one person or another to fabricate this affair around? And not only that, what about before the affair? That long middle period of your life, a time we all remember so well, when we were at home, when you and Daddy were there, every day, side by side, doing all the things parents do, presenting yourselves to us as married, content—*right?*

And what about that later time you've mentioned, when you and he were either back to back or sleeping in separate beds. What went on then? And how is it possible that these conflicts that distressed you so passed over our heads like clouds, changing the light for a moment or two, but never the landscape?

Not only that, I hear you say, but you told us to begin with that you wanted us to know you. But it's Daddy you've been talking about, telling us how he shut you out, how he ratted on you, how he lied to you. If that's to be said, shouldn't he say it?

And furthermore, to go back to you, Mama, have you done nothing all these years except think about him, curse him, yearn for him? My God, what a weird, dull life! No better than yearning for your married lover, was it?

I know, of course, that none of you in reality would ask these penetrating questions—you're too cautious, too loving. But you would think them—and others, I'm sure, that I haven't yet imagined. I will try to tell you, although I may in part have forgotten, what my life has been like.

Don't be alarmed. This is not to be our history, day by day and meal by meal, like the dull innocuous letters I used to write my mother, when our lives might perhaps be in crisis for any one of a number of reasons: "We had spinach and sour cream, roast beef, and green salad for Sunday lunch. I made a cheese-cake. Sunday afternoon we took the children swimming. Last night we played poker with . . ."   But there are a few things I should say.

First, during all the years from William's birth through Corinne's fifteenth year, it was they—you—who mattered, not just above all our personal affairs, but almost exclusively, leav-ing only the necessary chinks for our professional lives. We were raising children.

If, for a year or two, I was passionately, obsessively in love with him, fighting like a crusader at the walls of Jerusalem to breach the barriers between us, to open his heart to me, later, when the children began to come, tumbling out so quickly, so joyously, so demandingly, so tragically over the next eight years, I had neither the time nor the surplus strength and attention for "love affairs" with him or anyone. I remember that time as the time of warm flesh: of my body and his and yours, of aching episiotomies, burning hemorrhoids, of that first sweet painful fuck after childbirth and abstinence, of the drawing down of milk to the nipple and the long intimate hours of suckling; of dozing as I shook the crib of a screaming infant; of warm ammoniac babies at two years and three and four crawling into bed with us in the early morning hours, nestling between us; a time of rocking, singing, hugging, skipping, running, hopping, dancing, falling, swimming—jump to me! Jump! And then, later, of all the traumas, the crises—bloody noses, broken arms, lost glasses, speeding tickets, wrecked cars —the joys, the necessary boredom and rage and anxiety and excitement of raising children. No one had time for anything else.

It must be, too, that during those years George made over-tures to me, read aloud to me a poem that reduced him to tears, felt for me a passion the nature of which he tried to, but could not communicate:

" 'Come to the window, sweet is the night air!' "

Or, " 'In such a night/ Stood Dido with a willow in her hand/ Upon the wild sea banks, and waft her love/ to come again to Carthage.' "

It may even be that the very thing I had yearned for—the poem that he felt revealed his deepest longings—filled me with rage. *Another poem.*

But we were friends. Friends with an ongoing project, an ongoing responsibility, an ongoing mutual obsession. I suppose that's how it was.

All my—our—other concerns shrank beside these to less than nothing. Probably I would not have dreamed of leaving him, even if he had altogether quit sleeping with me. He was a good father. He loved you. You needed him. He needed you. I would have stayed and, perhaps, made other arrangements.

No doubt, too, one is—or rather, in those days one used to be—held firmly in these decisions by a network of friends and relatives who regarded divorce as the next thing to sodomy, as well as by one's own memories of a stable, nurtured childhood. But mainly, I think, I was sunk, immersed, in a dream of sex and mothering.

It was when the house began to clear out, to echo its emptiness that— No, that's not true. I've never felt the house was empty. I've had my work. You've come and gone.

What is true is that I did occasionally look with desire at other men. There was the Frenchman who spent a couple of months here in the late fifties studying some procedure or other at the University Hospital. There was George's and my good friend Harry Trent, poor fellow. He'd grown up with us and gone to med school with G. Then some thorn entered his flesh, dripped its poison into his veins, and he took to drink. His wife divorced him. It was then, when he began to regard the world with an ironic eye, when he embraced his own vulnerability, that he became dangerously attractive to me. He thought I was beautiful. (In those days I wore my hair twisted up into a Psyche knot with little curls escaping around my face and he said I had a profile like a girl on a Grecian urn.) Also he liked to talk to me. But unfortunately he stayed drunk most of the time and died young of cirrhosis.

Later, after everybody got through the civil rights period, there was a youngish black resident in surgery—oh, the fascinating, the forbidden mystery of black flesh—who used to come out and spend evenings with us. He loved poetry, too.

But you can see the problem. These men were George's friends and colleagues. I was not "liberated" enough to pursue them and they, under the circumstances, were unlikely to make the first move toward me, even when, as it seemed to me, my pent-up lust must have been as evident as the scarlet buttocks of a mandrill.

As for the faculty at the college, I sometimes meet someone whom I look forward to seeing between classes, to drinking coffee with, but no one who has stirred my blood.

I stop now and try to imagine what probing, cautiously worded questions James and Corinne might ask me here. William is not much of a questioner.

But I believe all three of you would listen or read on without a word, even though alarm bells have been going off in your heads, sirens howling in your ears. You are distressed, you want to hear me out; but you don't want to say one word that will bring you down in judgment either on me or on your father, one word that I could interpret as disloyal to him, as putting you in collusion with me against him. And of course you are right.

Finally, one summer I spent a couple of weeks on the coast with an old friend from college days and met there a man with whom I wanted to begin an affair. I wanted, I think, even more than sex or excitement or admiration, a companion. I was lonely, lonely, and companionship between men and women is almost impossible without sex. This was during the long period between when George quit sleeping with me and when I found out about his affair—very late, you see. I was already pushing sixty. How ridiculous it is to want to begin an affair—one's first extramarital affair—at sixty! My notion—technique of offering myself to him—was probably very like Marcel's aunts' painfully delicate, insanely unobtrusive technique of thanking Swann for the wine he brought them. Like them, perhaps, I believe that no one should be embarrassed by enthusiastic thanks—or by unwanted sexual overtures. In any case, whether he recognized the overtures or not I don't know, but he didn't respond.

So there you have, with one exception, equally abortive, the history of my abortive attempts to make a connection with a man in those lonely years. I'll come to the exception later.

Tuesday Sept. 16th

Again, although it's true that all the information I've been writing down is relevant to our predicament, I have been using it—the way I use moving the hose and pulling weeds between the bricks—to put off.

It was not The Toad. There was no near discovery in the mission church. It was someone else, somewhere else.

George cares about his work, but he hates his profession. Also, although he wants to be comfortable, he hates to make money. And doctors can't avoid making a great deal of money —far more than they need or deserve. What he has done about his dilemma over the years is as follows:

To begin with, he has consistently made bad investments. For example, at one point, he put all our savings into a franchise for a farm implement company. As partner in the scheme he took in a man who, he said, would furnish the business sense. As manager, they hired a "go-getter." Within five years the businessman and the go-getter had stolen the business from George. He had his attention on other things.

The device they used was quite simple and legal. After a couple of years the go-getter persuaded them to deal him in on the partnership. G. and his partner each sold him ten percent of their stock. It was only fair, George said. Besides, it was the only way they could keep him. After a couple more years, the partner and the go-getter made a short trip to the headquarters of the implement company and had the renewal of the franchise put in their names alone. They then explained to George that he could either take what they offered him for his stock, or he could force a sale of the buildings and equipment, in which case he would get even less. This is known as the manipulation of a minority interest.

These men's names are Melton Wetzger and Peter Parsons. There they are, exposed in their greed and shame—if they are still alive—to whoever reads this record.

Of course I know they're alive. But they're old now, *old.*

56

Maybe they have varicose veins and hematomas. Maybe they're bedridden with strokes or have had their legs cut off because of diabetic gangrene and are in the charge of callous, mindless sitters. Do they need punishment from me, for Christ's sake? So of course those are not their names. Not at all. Not even their initials.

To continue, George has invested over the years in hotels that have fallen down, wholesale grocery businesses that have gone bankrupt and cattle that have starved in a drought. What he is interested in is patching people up, not making money.

Now, it's almost impossible for a doctor to throw away his money fast enough to stay poor, so he has also given it away. Here, in my view, his judgment has been better. The causes he chooses may seem lost (feeding the starving, saving the whales) or almost lost (conserving the water table, abandoning nuclear power), but at least it's not because they are in the charge of crooks or drunkards or idiots.

But wealth is not the only consideration that has driven George away from his profession. He decided some years ago —and now, of course, there are innumerable studies to back him up—that doctors and hospitals were killing people. His practical response to this realization was to stand in the hospital door, so to speak, and send people away. That's how he got into emergency medicine.

At fifty-five—a reasonably competent general surgeon—he gave up surgery. Now, for a couple of twenty-four-hour shifts a week he does what used to be done by poverty-stricken interns—patches people up after fires and wrecks and falls, pumps out their stomachs, cuts the fishhooks out of their fingers, shocks them out of cardiac arrest, pops the Ping-Pong ball out of their throats. And then, if it's humanly, professionally, ethically possible, he sends them home to recover in a less dangerous environment than a hospital swarming with streptococci and hospital hepatitis and staffed by the Fausts of the modern world.

He's not quite so hipped on this as a young man I heard of

who works in an outpatient clinic at Peter Bent Brigham in Boston. He sits in his little cubicle of an office for X number of hours a week and simply sends people away: No, no. You don't need an antibiotic. Those things upset the bacterial balance in your intestines and turn your teeth yellow. No hemorrhoidectomy—go home and sit in a hot tub. Of course you don't want to have those vertebrae fused. Are you crazy? Go home. Go home. Go home! You'll live to be a hundred if you quit smoking, eat a balanced diet with plenty of roughage, stay off the freeways, look both ways before you cross the street, and laugh a lot.

Friday Sept. 26th

So it was in the emergency room that George met him—the young man he fell in love with.

None of you know him, or, if you ever did, you would not remember him—a timid, pudgy, self-conscious, probably unloved child, who, like Chuchundra, the Musk-rat in "Rikki-Tikki-Tavi," scurried along the walls of the room, while you shouted and tumbled and postured in the middle.

Let me tell you to begin with what he looks like. Like The Toad, he is short. Sometimes I think George is just sick of looking at me eyeball to eyeball—or, when I dress up and wear high heels, eyeball to nose. But that may be my nuttiness. I chose The Toad for my imaginary lover partly because her height is a quality that makes her like this real man. Their shortness signifies to me something deep in George's yearning heart. What is it? I can't put my finger on it. That— That he chooses at last, for the one to whom, after a lifetime closed off from those who love him, to open his life to, someone uneducated, limited, desperately, fatally flawed and wounded, ill, feeble—small.

He's a doctor, after all. Doctors have chosen, to begin with, a profession in which they are always standing up, patients lying down; they are strong, patients weak; they know, patients are ignorant. Doctors have, by definition of their situation, to be in charge, directing.

Who or what, then, threatened George so deeply that he chooses to deal with the weak, that he cannot risk himself, open his heart to his colleagues, his peers, his children—to me?

Well, enough facile psychologizing for the moment. The facts are that this man was a lab technician; that at the time

59

of the beginning of the affair he was James's age—twenty-six; that he was about as screwed up as you can get—on and off drugs, etc.—that George could do an intellectual two-and-a-half off the three-meter board before he got his swimming trunks pulled up; that George's friendship was, must have been, to begin with, the most fascinating thing that had ever happened to him—he must have been dazzled. George pointing out the constellations and the planets, humming snatches of Scarlatti, naming fauna and flora, recognizing old movie stars on TV, lecturing on Freud and Jung, recounting the gory or comical details of old emergency-room crises, identifying insects, malignant and benign, and reciting poetry, reciting poetry.

That's not what I believed to begin with, but it's what I believe now—maybe. He was dazzled.

I started out to tell you what he looked like. Short, I said, and got no farther. He is slight—not an excess pound on him now, pale-skinned, fair-haired, has the unhealthy pallor of indoor people. A good if fragile-looking profile, beautiful large dark eyes, intelligent and expressive. Or they were before he knew I knew—afterwards they were evasive. He has that striking coloring that old-fashioned ladies used to call "chatain"— tawny, reddish blond hair and dark brown eyes.

George brought him to the house half a dozen times. He was "helping him work out his problems." He's undertaken similar projects over the years with a dozen or more lost souls—always young souls, I note now—has been the confidant of friends of the children's, of nursing students, of interns. But he doesn't usually bring them home. This one, weirdly, he wanted me to know.

"He's bright," he said. And then occasionally he would pass on to me the boy's comments: "He's a bit shy around you. Says you're so smart." "He thinks you're pretty."

Smart! Pretty! If sixty years in this vale of tears have left me smart and pretty, I must be simple-minded. You can see I already smelled a rat.

But before I really smelled the rat, the affair had probably been going on for months.

Then it happened. It was not that George touched him. He laid his hand on George's shoulder—an unthinkable familiarity.

They were standing in the open doorway, facing each other. He was leaving the house, George had walked to the door with him, and he laid his hand on George's shoulder.

Sirens went off in my head. Danger! Fire! Explosives!

I should say here, I believe, something else that I had observed, before the boy laid his hand on George's shoulder. George was happy. Something was happening to make him—not content, but happy: joyous. He was full of trivial conversation, came home with more than the usual local gossip and talk of emergency-room problems, wanted to read aloud, recited poetry morning, noon, and night.

I would hear his voice above the shower, mumbling through his shaving cream—" 'Weep no more, woeful Shepherds weep no more,' " hear him whistling as he set off, in a far greater hurry than was his custom, to do his shift in the emergency room.

I want to tell you something of the boy's circumstances.

Saturday Sept. 27th

Sometimes, when I get up after a sleepless night, I am sure
I have, in fact, slept, have dreamed all night of being awake.
With this dream, presumably, I punish myself for not staying
awake and being miserable during some particularly excruciating crisis. Or is it that I'm always dreaming, only sometimes
—daily—I dream that I'm not dreaming?

I dream in color. I have the power to bring back old dreams
and run them through again, like memories, even sometimes,
like memories, give them another ending. Over the years, in
my sleep, I have lived through again and again my frustrating
early love affair. He gets a divorce, we build a life together. Or
he has rejected me, vanished, reappears for a passionate reunion.

The Senoi are right, of course. The night world, a third of
one's life, those—for me at this age—twenty sleeping years,
swarming with tragedy, passion, adventure, are not less real
than the other two-thirds—more real surely than the huge
blocks one loses. (What happened to 1956, for example?) More
real than standing empty-headed on a street corner waiting for
a bus, more real than driving to the campus, arriving there, and
finding one can't recall which route one followed, more real
than the hours of double solitaire, the forgotten plane trips, the
endless unconscious hours of grading papers, sitting in faculty
meetings.

I woke last night in a state of acute anxiety, pulled my body
against George's, squeezed myself close to him.

Help! Help!

I had had a dream in which my brother was visiting us. He
was admiring a small wood carving that George had bought,

62

holding it in his hand. I was nervous—the carving was fragile, George prized it, I knew. My brother is clumsy. I held out my hand for it.

I see the carving clearly: It was the figure of a man, four or five inches tall, dressed in light blue bib overalls, wearing a yellow straw farmer's hat, holding a pitchfork (shades of Freud and Norman Rockwell), precisely, sharply, perfectly carved and painted. My brother put it in my hand. I was holding it carefully, turning it this way and that for him to admire, and it fell apart. The arms and legs fell off, the hat slid down over the face.

Oh, George, hold me, forgive me. I've broken it. I didn't mean to, but I've broken it.

It was *my* dream.

Later

The boy's circumstances.

He was divorced, had two children by a marriage contracted when he was eighteen or nineteen. The woman got pregnant on purpose, George told me once, to trap him. This, of course, the boy must have told him. My conclusion with regard to his character was that he had no scruples about slandering the mother of his children. But give him credit for one thing. He felt a responsibility toward the children, contributed to their support, spent time with them.

Now he lived a radically different life, with a woman and another man—friends, George said—for the obvious and necessary purpose of pooling rent and sharing expenses. "I suppose one of them sleeps with the woman," he said at the beginning, with a crafty semblance of indifference. "I don't know which one. Both, maybe."

I had seen the house before I went to it the first time, passed it occasionally on errands into the same part of town as the Salvation Army and Toad's mission church; that run-down, middle-class-slipping-into-a-slum neighborhood where two- and three-bedroom cottages built during the twenties and thirties rent for two and three and even four hundred dollars a month.

I don't know how people live these days. How can you pay three hundred dollars a month for one of those houses, how can you live—shoe clerks, A&P checkers?

Yes, I've seen it. Not only seen it—have been inside, once with George, once alone. I'll come shortly to both these occasions.

To continue: He'd had a couple of years of college before marriage had forced his nose to the grindstone. He wanted to go back, "to better himself," George said, maybe even to study medicine, but given the circumstances of his life, how could he? The two years he'd had in one of our less than adequate community colleges were technician's training, not even transferable to a university. He had the obligation of support money to the children. His father was dead, his mother worked. There was no money anywhere. He was trapped.

I cringed. I'd never heard George use such a phrase as "better himself." My tongue ached at the root to say, "You mean he's not good enough? Not good enough for what? For whom?" And also: "Would you recommend medicine to him —to anyone—as a career?" Instead I said, reasonably, "Well, of course, lots of people work their way through premed and med school, but it takes time."

Not only that, G. said, he'd left school under a cloud. Something about a near-conviction for selling dope.

What else?

His eyes sometimes had the wild look I've seen in the eyes of squirrels trapped in the humane box traps put out to combat the burgeoning squirrel population in our city. (We've had a couple of cases of attacks on people by rabid squirrels.) It was as if he restrained himself from chattering, hurling himself against the wire.

"Is he an addict?" I said. "To what?"

"No, no, Corinne. You've got it wrong. He smoked a lot of dope those first two years and sold some to pay for his own. It was all blown way out of proportion. You haven't forgotten already, have you, that kids went to prison five years ago for possession of an ounce of marijuana with intent to sell?"

He went on. "He doesn't think with notable logic—tends to feel vaguely guilty—who knows why? He told me once that he married because his wife was a good influence on him, kept him 'in line.' She's very strait-laced—belongs to one of those Pentecostal churches, I think, or is a charismatic Baptist or something."

He paused. Then, thoughtfully: "He sometimes contradicts himself. What worries me is that he strikes me as being at the edge of serious trouble. Some days he comes in to work— It's curious, he's always happy, smiling, but he has no access to his own feelings." (Oh, George!) "His happiness seems to me to mask—this sounds melodramatic, I know—despair. He may be suicidal. I think a receptive ear, a little support . . . I might help him."

George is arrogant, I suppose—or used to be. Thought he could sew up a soul as neatly as he sews up a split lip.

I thought that one of two things must be true. Either G. was showering him with gifts—George loves to give presents to people he cares about, never forgets birthdays, takes basketsful of vegetables from his garden to friends and relatives —or else he, the boy, was setting George up for blackmail. It might even be that he and his housemates or the ex-wife were in collusion.

Remember that at this time George and I had had no sex for more than a year, that we lived in a curious, cut-off, piecemeal friendship, which was to me like . . .

I can scarcely even remember what it was like. In a way, as I've said, it was like being stuck in an iceberg. But of course there were all kinds of complex mitigating circumstances. In human terms we were committed, after all, to our children, our familial responsibilities, our shared past, our financial partnership; able to trust each other in all these areas without reserva-

65

tion—not to be right or clever, but to be scrupulous, to act with regard to each other's interests.

I had looked around me at marriages more than once and knew how rare this kind of trust was.

And then, besides, George had said it was all on account of his prostate trouble.

But at the same time, with all this trust, with all my sympathy for his alleged condition, we were closed against each other and we hated each other. That is, I hated him, although I didn't fully realize it until I fell in love with him again. He says he never hated me, but I don't believe him. I know. Somewhere, at the bottom, everyone hates everyone.

Remember, too, that, as I've said, George tends to lay himself open to exploitation. He had never, so far as I knew, had any extramarital relationship, let alone a homosexual one. He was fifty-eight, the boy twenty-seven. How could I not be hysterical with anxiety?

I thought. I thought.

Granted I felt a certain painful exhilaration: At last the wall would be breached. We would come to know each other.

But—danger! I was, I *was* concerned for him. Had he tipped over? And, if he hadn't, if he loved the boy, had found his true sexual identity, what anguish was he laying himself open to? What punishment?

To begin with I thought: Let him go his way for a while. Watch. Wait. But then, soon, anxiety and exhilaration began to try to take over the reins. How vulnerable he was! Fifty-eight and he'd never in all the years of our marriage even looked at another woman.

That, too, pierced me to the heart. Of course he'd never looked at another woman. What he'd wanted all these years without having sense enough to know it (or, even worse, unthinkable, knowing it, suppressing it, fighting it, using me to fight it) had been, not me, not any woman, but a man. I'd lived my whole life trying to please a man who had been using every ounce of energy he could harness to deny to himself that he preferred assholes to vaginas.

66

Mama! Mama! Stop! Are you talking to us? We mustn't hear this. Hush. Hush!

No. I'm talking to myself, to him, to the world. And I'll go on. I will go on.

There may be a segment in this account, like the chapter in *Tristram Shandy* devoted entirely to punctuation, into which I will put all the sexual fantasies, all the explicit sex—get it out of the way. Read on, then, anticipating. When you come to it, if you don't like explicit sex, you can skip it. If you do, perhaps I'll arrange the pages so they can be clipped out and moved around to the appropriate places and reinserted.

It just occurred to me, I might include an additional challenge, the element of a puzzle: Which episode goes where?

Thursday Oct. 2nd

You can see by the date that I've been away from my desk for almost a week.

Where am I? Where were we?

Or, and here I feel as if I may be slipping into a waking dream, how can I be sure what happened next? Time has passed. A year? Two years? Maybe I've changed the order of events, even the content of events inside my own head, thinking, I'll put off telling about this until later. Later it'll be easier, more probable, truer . . . Or, this is too embarrassing, that intolerable. Some small alteration is necessary and will make no difference.

What I must do is proceed methodically, chronologically into this desperate enterprise, proceed morning after morning —perhaps even proceed truthfully.

I am thinking, trying to remember.

Truthfully, I think what happened next, before I talked to George about what I believed—what I *knew*—before I confronted the boy, was that we went to that house.

Now I am not unacquainted with the lairs of the young. I have visited each of you in your first apartments. I remember, James, the apartment you used to share with Big Foot, who never washed out the coffeepot and had his collection of three hundred army adventure paperbacks stashed on a narrow shelf in the top of the one closet, where they fell out on my head every time I opened the door to get my coat. And I know, William, that you still open the icebox, stand, staring in, and eat, like a great parrot, a meal consisting entirely of fruit. You even sometimes stand on one foot and cock your head, listening to melodies I can't hear, while you nibble delicately at a

68

mango. Meanwhile, I'm sitting politely, quietly in the background while my stomach screams *Meat! Meat!*

And you, Corinne. You're obsessively neat now that you have children—if you weren't, of course, you'd be buried under their toys, spend your life looking for lost Darth Vaders, missing pieces of the Lego set, odd socks and gloves. But I can remember when your closet was empty and all your clothes piled on chairs.

None of you went in much for the styles of the sixties or early seventies, perhaps because you were a year or two too young, but rather, I think, because you tend to go your own eccentric ways. No black lights, bead curtains, water pipes, or water beds for you. But various of your friends and my students affected counterculture styles, and so I am used to that genre, too.

But I was ill-prepared for this house.

The circumstances of our visit (G.'s and mine) were as follows:

But wait.

First, our own house. George loves our house and, off and on, so do I. It had once belonged to his great-grandparents, and when we moved back here after his surgical residency, we bought it from the estate of a recently dead cousin. He refinished the worn random oak flooring himself, repaired the old egg-and-dart cornices, screened the big back porch . . .

But the town first. I'll put the house in the town. It could be Shreveport or Jackson or Macon or Montgomery—any small Southern city or large Southern town. There are here, still, a few shreds of evidence left of its pre-Civil War existence, a few houses preserved by the local historical society or owned by new money; but mostly, as it now stands, it was built in two or three surges: during the eighteen eighties, again during the tens and twenties of this century, and lately, during the long groundswell of change, prosperity, convulsion, and destruction in the fifties, sixties, and seventies—our lifetime. Of course, there are still a few "old" families left—some fallen on hard times, living out their Faulknerian or Williamsian eccentric

69

dooms and dreams, some growing fat and genial on royalties from the natural gas and oil that has been discovered under their worn-out land. But mostly we are all neatly fitted together in the new national jigsaw puzzle: There are the McDonald's and towboat tycoons in their $500,000 French Provincial manor houses with slate mansard roofs. There are the middle-aged doctors and lawyers in their fake Georgian and Louisiana plantation houses, the academics "with incomes" in elegantly refurbished late Victorians, the young professionals who are slowly refurbishing their own, the black bureaucrats and professionals who are rapidly taking over what we used to call . . . This is turning out to be the architectural, anthropological, and demographic section (like the upcoming sex section), clearly not meant, Corinne, for you and your brothers or for you, George, but for a more general audience, which needs to fix some notion in its head of where and how we live. To go on, the black professionals who are taking over what we used to call the Lake Gardens ghetto—a middle-middle-class white suburb that always went a hundred percent with the Republican party, the Baptist church, the private (seg) schools, even, at its lunatic fringes, with the KKK.

And then there are the old parts of town backed against the levee. Once we were a real river town, on a narrow, delightful green river named the Ouachita or the Pearl or the Big Black; but now there are locks above and below our city. Sometimes what was the river flows north, sometimes south. It is scummed with diesel fuel from unloading towboats and has turned a dead opaque gray color. Oily rainbows shimmer on its gray surface, but no fish rise from its lethal depths. Anyhow, the old parts of town, lying in the curve of the levee, are lower-middle-class white slums on the north and black slums on the south, with a few old houses like ours still standing here and there, far back in wide yards, surrounded by walls or iron fences. And of course all around the edges are the projects and the grain elevators, the rug factories and the compresses and the oil mills.

An illuminated cross stretching north and south, east and

west, pins us to the map—the strips. From the air, at night, coming in by plane from Memphis or New Orleans or Atlanta, it is a true jeweled cross, six lanes of moving, twinkling lights, set on either side with rows of neon rubies and sapphires and emeralds and topaz—the neon of Wendy's and Harry's Disco and Long John Silver's Sea Food Shoppe—and strung with loops of yellow sodium streetlights.

Coming in by car, by day, as I often do from symposia or workshops or professional meetings—yes, I still have a professional life, although clearly at the moment I am devoting little of my energy and attention to it. Teaching, to me, like medicine to George, has come to seem a farcical profession. Coming in by day, then, I see it in a less glittering setting, particularly at this time of year. August has moved now into early October. Grackles are walking on my lawn picking at the ground around the scarlet clumps of surprise lilies. I come to my home through the heavy poisonous Southern twilight, heavier, deadlier than the fumes of Los Angeles smog.

October. They—we—are defoliating the cotton. The bowl of the land is full to the brim with poison. The earth reeks like a huge silage trench, like a ripped open grave, reeks of rotting vegetation, of death. The beacon, the tower I first see when I drive down into the bowl, used to be the steeple of an old Catholic church. But now the spire is dwarfed by the cylindrical tower of our power company generating station (AP&L, MP&L, GP, take your choice), its sunbright aircraft-warning blinker as blinding as the flame of a welding torch, its plume of deadly sulfurous smoke stretching from horizon to horizon. This is our home.

I began, though, inside another beginning, to tell you about our house. We bought it, as I said, twenty-five years ago from a cousin's estate, one of those old-fashioned story-and-a-half cottages with dormers front and back and wide latticed porches, the kind one used to see in every old Southern town. It even has a detached wing—what used to be the kitchen and

71

carriage house, and above them, the "garçonnière" where adolescent males could pursue their nocturnal lives without disturbing their mothers' dreams. We turned the carriage house and kitchen into a double garage and use the upstairs for storage. There the children held their secret-society meetings and played on rainy days. The house backs up to the levee and is surrounded by a ragged big yard—plenty of room for baseball and football games—the borders full of ancient azaleas and camellias and the perennials one doesn't have to look after—swamp iris, day lilies, hydrangeas. Neither George nor I has much time for yard work, but we chop at it sporadically—cut back the poison ivy and bignonia and trumpet vines, pull out the privet and euonymus, spray the camellias a couple of times a year for scale.

Inside, though— You know, children, what it's like inside, how comfortably ours, so I won't give you a *House and Garden* tour, but say only that it is a house full of books and music and light, full of green light, moving light; the windows (placed, as they are in all those old houses, so that the Gulf breeze sweeps through from south to north) opening everywhere on the wavering leaf patterns of old trees, the green slope of the levee. The shadows of the leaves move softly on the bare floors in the summer, their reflections shimmer in the mirrors.

In bed, on a summer morning, after twenty-five years, it still gives me the profoundest joy to wake and look out my bedroom window into those green moving masses of light and shadow.

So he took me to the boy's house.

The boy.

He's not a boy, of course, but a man, divorced, the father of two children.

He . . .

I cannot write his name. I cannot bear to speak his name. I think of giving him a name like "The Toad"—The Technician, for example. That's his trade. No, I'll call him Chuchundra—The Musk-rat. Once a timid, chubby musk-rat pup, now a lean, roaming, scavenging, hungry musk-rat male, who hides himself in order to survive, who knows it's eat or be eaten.

Do you understand that my hatred of him is entirely unjustified? My view of his character questionable?

No, that's not true.

Yes, it is.

I have to go on.

George had suggested to me quite openly, guilelessly, that he would like to give "them" (the boy and his housemates) some things for their house.

"We have that bed frame stored over the garage, the one James built for his apartment. Nobody's using it and he (the boy) is sleeping on a mattress on the floor."

"Sure," I said. "Of course. He's welcome to it."

"I thought we might *lend* it to him," he said, "in case James should ever want it back."

My heart, my uncontrollable insane heart began to pound as if I were in the twentieth mile of a marathon.

"And there are those framed prints in the hall closet," he said. "The Cézannes. The Winslow Homers that used to be in William's room before we got the Klees."

"Fine," I said.

"It may sound foolish," he said, "but he seems to me to have —I don't know—such a tenuous hold on his life . . . If he could make even one room into a place where he would like to be . . ."

So the boy came and helped George bring the bed frame down from the storage room and tie it on top of the car; and George got the pictures; and I smiled sincerely and the boy smiled sincerely and George smiled sincerely and, as they were getting ready to leave, the boy said sincerely, "Come on with us, Miss Corinne. I'd like you to see our place and meet my friends."

Miss Corinne! But it must not have come off for him, either. He never addressed me again by that name—or by any name. I suppose he found it as hard to name me as I to name him.

"Yes," George said. "Come on, Corinne."

So I went.

I think I went. Looking back, I find it hard to believe that my memory of going to his house is a memory of a real event in the temporal world. Maybe I dreamed I went.

The woman was sitting in the living room in the middle of a couch, cross-legged in a kind of Buddha pose, one of those maniacally smiling "laughing Buddhas." She nodded her head and bowed like the detective in an old Charlie Chan movie. What was she doing? What was she smiling at?

The boy introduced us. She, as it turned out, was a graduate student in the local community college—getting an M.A. in "personnel." She did not rise to welcome us to her house, but then so many young people don't do that any more.

The living room was wall-to-wall furniture, only the narrowest corridors left between tables and chairs. Maybe it all belonged to her. A whole set of Sears Mediterranean special. Even the bookcase had carved posts. A Sears floral print nylon rug covered the floor. Sears nylon curtains, solid blue with a metallic thread, glittered at the windows.

I sat down.

The boy got a hammer and nails and he and George hung the Winslow Homer prints over the "credenza." Then the two of them took the Cézannes into his bedroom.

Saliva ran in my mouth. I was afraid I might vomit. The woman and I looked at each other. I gathered my fragmented self together to speak.

"Do you— Do you know Dr. Speakes?" I said. "Such a nice fellow. He does something in your area, I think. Industrial psychology? I wish I knew more about those things."

"Yes," she said, smiling.

She was thick-waisted, heavy-breasted. Long dark brown hair was twisted up into a smooth knot exactly on top of her head. Were her earlobes elongated?

"Have you been at the college for long? I mean, did you do your undergraduate work here?"

"Yes," she said, smiling.

What am I doing here? Oh, what? Why, in these sorrowful circumstances, are we all smiling at one another?

Now, from the bedroom, we heard the sound of hammering.

"I'm in the—the . . ." I could not think of the name of my subject or my school. "I teach," I said distractedly, "at— at . . ."

She seemed to recognize dimly that she should speak. "I like to read," she said. "I read all the time. Georgette Heyer is my favorite writer."

"What?" I was staring at my delicate Homer prints of the Hudson River and its wooded banks, hanging above the credenza.

How can this be? I gazed deeply into the landscape. Maybe I can dream myself into it—into that blue-green wash below the rock there, that spot shadowed by a clump of birch trees.

"Georgette Heyer. Isn't she great? I've read every one of . . ." She trailed off, continued to smile like Charlie Chan.

"Yes," I said. "She's great, isn't . . ." What am I saying?

George and the boy come out of the bedroom. The three of them are talking. About what?

Someone—who? I can't stop staring into the woods, willing myself into the woods—puts a cold glass into my hand. I must have said yes to the offer of a drink. I raise it to my lips and taste a horrible sweet liquid. What is it? I never drink soft drinks. This must be, I suppose, some kind of cola. I set it on the table.

"I told you you didn't want . . ."

Is that George speaking?

"You never drink . . ."

"Thank you," I say to the boy. "Thank you."

"Have some trash . . ." He laughs as if he has made a joke. Trash?

"Thank you. Thank you."

Trash turns out to be a toasted mixture of cereal and nuts and seeds concocted by the woman. I crawl under the birch trees. I am lying on the cool mossy shadowy ground under the trees. I hear the sound of water running over stones.

And then we are gone, out of the house, driving home. We have left the clump of birches, the flowing river, the shadowy spot where I lay, left the pictures hanging over the credenza, left my two beautiful Cézannes hanging in his bedroom, over the bed James built, where they will look down from time to time on George and the boy fucking.

I cup my two hands and dream that I am holding in them the white-veined green stone of my Senoi dream, feel the weight of it in my hands.

"What's the matter with you?" George says. "Are you sick? You look strange."

"Yes, I think I am," I say. "Maybe I am coming down with something."

Monday Oct. 13th

If I concocted that excruciating, absurd story about George
and The Toad, made it up out of whole cloth, it must have
been for good reasons; and now that I look back at it, I know
that one of the reasons was not at all, as I wrote when I
confessed my duplicity, that I wanted to shield George's privacy, but that I couldn't bear to think about him with the boy.
And I can't, I still can't. I can't.

They surface in the waters of my imagination—I see them.
Oh, I see them—and I push them down again and again to
drown in the depths of my dreams.

Later

The black birds, the grackles, are walking decorously on the
grass near the clumps of scarlet lilies, bending their heads,
creaking, pecking. The sycamore leaves are sailing down, fleets
of sailing leaves . . .

I cannot, cannot bear it.

Later

When I told him I knew, we must have had a conversation
very like the one I said we had about him and The Toad. It's
hard for me to remember.

Not true. Not hard to remember. Hard to believe. It's the
stone of my life and I do not wish to—will not—carry it.

To begin with he denied it, said I was crazy; but he had lied
repeatedly, recklessly, and it was easy to back him into a corner.

Easy. Also necessary. Understand that even though I had

77

caught him in the lies, I was haunted, horrified, terrified by the possibility that I might be insane, that I might have made it all up. But of course there was the other danger that made openness essential.

"I thought about not telling you I knew," I said, "for a long time—weeks. But I decided it was too dangerous."

Again we are sitting in the living room, he in his usual place on the sofa, I in mine. I have a cup of coffee. Again he has drawn in his sprawled foot, folded his arms across his chest, is listening, alert, attentive, as if he might be at a lecture.

I am filled with anxiety, but at the same time I believe myself to be detached. We would behave like adults.

"Dangerous?" he said. "What are you talking about?"

"You're vulnerable," I said. "I make you vulnerable. There he is, you know. There they all are—the three of them—and the ex-wife, too. Neither you nor I know anything about any of them. And he's been in trouble already about dope. How could I be sure he wasn't setting you up somehow?"

"Setting me up!" A curious thing happened to his face, an indescribable expression crossed it, as if he moved deeper within himself to a place where I could not possibly follow him, to another world, another life in which I had absolutely no part. He concealed himself.

At that moment, I believe, my own obsession was born. I would follow him there. I would dig him out. He would be mine.

"Yes," I said. "He could—they could—any one of them or all of them together—be planning to blackmail you. They— he—could threaten to tell me. But if I know and you know I know, then they have no hold on you. I know you don't care what they might say to anyone else, anyone but me and the children. But you would try to keep from hurting us."

He shook his head. "They know nothing at all about it," he said, "and he . . ."

"It was something I had to take into account," I said. "I had to make sure you were safe from that. I would kill him, you know, without a qualm, a regret, if he did anything to damage you."

Again that look of retreating into himself. What does it mean? What secret ecstasy, ease, trust, friendship, what incommunicable fulfillment is he concealing out of the knowledge that the comparison of *him* and *me* would be mortally wounding to me? What does he not say to save me from his contempt for me, his pity?

He spoke as if he had not heard what I'd said about murder. "As for wanting something from me, he doesn't even like me to give him presents, even a birthday present. Nothing."

"Oh, George," I said, "I don't care if you spend money on him. I just don't care. What does that matter?"

"What do you want me to do?" he said. "I'll break it off. Do you want me to break it off?"

"What good will it do me if you break it off? It'll just make you hate me." I did know, I did, already, out of how deep, how inviolable a place in his nature this infatuation, obsession, love had welled up.

We were both silent. I could not think what to say, much less what to do. I could not think at all. He got up after a few minutes, walked over to the window, and stood with his back to me, looking out into the darkness. He stood there and in a little while, when he got out his handkerchief and wiped his face, I realized that he was weeping.

"George?" I said.

He didn't turn around. "I don't want to hurt you," he said.

I said nothing for a minute. Then: "Do you want a divorce?"

"A divorce! No. Of course not. I love you." He looked at me. "Do you?"

I shook my head.

"I'll break it off," he said again.

"You have to live your life," I said. "I want to want for you what you want for yourself."

How silly I was, children, how childish, how deluded. Have you read that age brings wisdom and detachment? Not true.

It brings passion, more passion, obsession, fury, frustration, as if one lived again through an adolescence that would open out not into maturity, but into oblivion. There was no need for the foolish whisky-sodden poet to address his ancient passion-battered father: "Do not go gentle into that good night." No need at all.

The urgent next thing to say is that as a result of my telling George that I knew, he and I began sleeping together again.

Wednesday Oct. 15th

He was consumed with guilt, and it was not because The M-r was a man, but because he'd betrayed me—he had come to terms, he explained, with his own nature. To exorcise the guilt, to keep me pacified, he was loving and attentive. And I —I was tender and tolerant and understanding.

All this, of course, is behavior appropriate to what is known as open marriage. And open marriage can be achieved. People who really care about each other are supposed to be able to achieve it—to care and let go. I have read this repeatedly in do-it-yourself psychology books and been assured by smiling understanding therapists—yes, I had a fling at that, too—that it is true. Besides, it has an ancient and orthodox ring, doesn't it? ". . . and thy neighbor as thyself," etc.

I remember very well, because I have a residual tic to remind me of it, how sincerely, earnestly I went about "working through" my old resentments, my old hatreds, in order freely to let him go his way. The tic comes from a period when I was trying out do-it-yourself Gestalt. I practiced all the chewing and swallowing exercises, revolting though they were—gagged over my breakfast as I chewed and chewed and chewed my life and swallowed it down. Then I started the series in which you learn to relax the diaphragm and belly muscles and let out all the repressed sobs—and repressed orgasms. I sobbed enough for all of you put together, my dears—and for the babies, too; but I did not, in fact, become wiser or more tolerant thereafter. Instead I acquired such a relaxed belly that now at night, in bed, those muscles occasionally jump without warning.

"What's the matter with you?" George will say, lying beside me, his arm across me. "What's happening to your belly? You jerk like you have incipient Parkinsonism."

But that was later. To begin with, he felt guilty and I reassured him. Oh, everything was open now, grand. I was tender and understanding. He, in his love for me, in his guilt and gratitude, his need to keep me pacified and the affair humming along on its own track, was increasingly gentle, considerate, talkative, attentive. We danced around each other in a frenzy of mutual affection and consideration. For the moment it was true, at least a part of what I had hoped for, longed for years ago. Or so it appeared. He was open with me, open with himself.

And as the days passed, all this affection began for me to have in it an element of desire.

Understatement. What happened was that as soon as he wanted someone else, I was no longer capable of the kind of friendship we'd had, with all its abysses of misunderstanding, its walls of privacy, its piercing wounds of rejection. I wanted him. I wanted him to want only me. A spasm of possessiveness seized me that was as physical as the contractions of childbirth.

No. Wait.

That came later, after we began to sleep together again. Get it all straight, for Christ's sake. Try to tell the truth.

One day, after we'd danced our minuet of understanding and affection for some weeks, after I'd opened my arms to him, laid his dear head on my breast, cherished him, crawled into bed with him again, given and received the brotherly, sisterly caresses that assuaged our mutual distress, he said, "I'd like for us to make love again. Do you think . . . ?"

And I, deep in my drive to accept, to love wholly, without reservation, to do what everybody from Buddha and Jesus to Frederick Perls has said in one way or another that it's possible to do, said without a moment's hesitation, "Yes."

I would go all the way, would follow this tunnel in my life to whatever place it led, deeper into the rock, under the ground, along the side of whatever underground river, in whatever darkness, opening out into whatever abyss or green meadow.

That was what I thought.

Thought is the wrong word. Surely, I did not have a single thought in any part of my reasonably functional brain. But this is what I was childish enough to believe: I believed that I would be generous, would release him; that I would show him my love, would bare every corner of my life to him and, then, as a result, he would not want the boy, The Musk-rat, anymore. He would want me, only me, only me, only me.

Later

But if you were inside this iceberg, as you say you were, why did you care whether he wanted you or not?

When you're rearranging pages, perhaps one block of the explicit sex should go here. It could read as follows: Here is a way, children (you may already have hit upon it for yourselves), to keep yourselves awake on long solitary drives, if, like me, you have occasionally to get up at five or six in the morning, drive two hours or more, work your way through a business day. With me it may be a symposium on the modern novel ("Where Are We Going?") or a meeting of the MLA, where I have to listen to three or four usually dull papers and talk to my colleagues about this or that Byzantine aspect of academic politics. It's on the drive home that I get sleepy. I've had a couple of drinks and eaten dinner at the Holiday Inn and I can barely keep my eyes open.

You masturbate. The challenge of bringing yourself to a climax and at the same time keeping your eye on the road is guaranteed to keep you alert. Wakes you up more thoroughly than a cup of coffee or a piece of ice on the back of the neck, takes less time than pulling off in a roadside park for a nap.

Never mind concealing yourselves from me, children. I see you exchanging glances: Our mother—our sensible, comical, reserved, but never unpredictable mother—has turned out in her old age to be a sex maniac. What on earth shall we do with her?

83

No. Let me continue.

If you are driving home to an eager husband or wife or lover, you may not want to take the edge off your appetite. In this case, as an effective substitute, I recommend ice on the back of the neck and an open window with the cold wind blowing in.

But such, at that time, was not the case with me.

I tell you this by way of illustrating that the iceberg I was encased in was rotten in spots, had some deep fissures in it.

So it took only a very little tenderness, a very little sexual attention to melt it as completely as if he had directed a laser beam at it.

Besides, I loved him.

Now what?

We did begin to make love again, tentatively, carefully, cautiously.

For me a dam almost two years in the building burst with a roaring rush that left me filled one day with the ecstasy of a sixteen-year-old bride, the next with the fury of Ariadne abandoned.

For a long time it was as if I were riding a roller coaster from which no matter how I tried, no matter what I willed, I could not get down. It may be that I am still aboard.

I see myself, like those miserable freaks who try to break the record on the roller coaster at Coney Island, riding night and day for weeks, months. I am exhausted, frantic, determined, hanging on to the side bars of my carriage, my face burning in the wind.

But those freaks, the ones trying to break the record, can call out at the starting station and stop the train if they like, can't they? Not I.

Below me, now and then, I catch glimpses of faces in the crowd, watching me, half amused, half indifferent, wondering how long the show will last.

And George? Where is he? There he is with the boy, The Musk-rat. They've bought cotton candy and are holding the huge pink puffs up to their open mouths for another bite.

I reach out and snatch him aboard.

Poor George.

With the best intentions—indeed, courageously—he had offered himself to me again. And I snatched him up and flung him aboard this careening, destinationless train.

Things got worse for me.

He had his times to see the boy. Genially, maturely, I said good-bye to him, saw him off on the afternoons they spent together. Then I did all sorts of things.

Some days I would take the car out on the False River Road and drive that flat straight ten-mile stretch as fast as I could make the car go. I have an eight-year-old BMW, a good car, and on days like that I have driven it as fast as a hundred and twenty miles an hour.

Some days I wandered through the desert of the malls, gazing in the windows of Zales' at the rows and rows of engagement rings with their minute chip settings, at the racks hung with golden hearts on flimsy golden chains and silver slave bracelets all ready to be engraved with the initials of lovers; into the cases at Cheese Heaven jammed with wheels of Port Salud, great round Edams, pungent Italian sausages.

Or I took the car to the car wash. For some reason I like to wash and wax the car, although I am not a car freak. I like it, I suppose, for the same reason that I like to piece together old records or put up pickles, because it is solitary, repetitive, brainless work. And I no longer had any pleasure in pickling, in watering, in weeding. I cared nothing any more for our house, our yard. Nothing was ours. His "ours" was invested in the boy. The car is mine.

I was teaching, but between semesters, during holidays, I spent a great deal of time on the road—went to Atlanta to see Corinne, to south Alabama to see James, to the coast again to see my friend from college days. I held William in reserve. I would go, soon, to see him.

Alone in the house, as I sometimes was those afternoons, I got crazier and crazier. The reason . . .

I suppose I'll never know, never understand the reason, reasons. All I can do is report how I felt, what I did.

It became more and more difficult for me to sleep through a night. At two or three I would get up, turn on the television set in the kitchen, at the opposite end of the house from our bedroom, and watch old movies until four or five in the morning. James Cagney, George Raft, Ingrid Bergman, Edward G. Robinson, James Stewart, Katharine Hepburn, Margaret Sullavan drifted furiously, passionately across the screen, while I sat at the kitchen table sipping a cup of hot milk—hot milk in the stomach draws the blood from the brain, induces sleep—vaguely aware of their presence, their ghostly rages and partings, reunions and deaths. At four or five I would go back to bed, get up at eight, and stagger off to meet a class.

I would wander, some nights, out under the gray trees, gray leaves whispering, moving above me in the moving night air, would walk around and around the perimeter of the yard to tire myself out, find myself standing in the middle of the garage planning a reorganization of the tool closet, a clearing out of the upstairs storage rooms: I would get rid of everything and then go.

One night I found myself in the big can and preserve closet in the kitchen, sitting on the floor in the corner, shelves filled with guava jelly and fig preserves stacked above my head to the ceiling, mops and brooms in their racks against the wall beside me. I had pulled my knees against my chest and huddled there, like a child put in the closet by a vengeful stepmother. Outside the closet on the kitchen counter a snarling James Cagney confronted for the millionth time a snarling Edward G. Robinson. Or maybe it was Margaret Sullavan, heroically giving up her lover. Or Bette Davis going blind. Voices from a gray box, shadows on a gray screen.

I am suffering. Why, why am I suffering? What am I doing here in this closet, this house, this life?

Saturday Oct. 18th

When my mother was pregnant with my younger sister and forced to stay in bed most of the time because she was threatened with a miscarriage, she sent me to stay with my aunt and her new husband. I was only three and I remember nothing of that visit, but I have been told by my mother that I stayed four months—the last three of her pregnancy and the first of my sister's life—and that when I got home, I did not recognize either her or my father, clung instead to my uncle-in-law and was, of course, necessarily, torn away from my moorings again.

When I was six, I was sent away for the summer, this time so that my mother could put all her attention on my sister, who was "desperately" ill with what used to be called acidosis—could keep nothing on her stomach and kept getting dehydrated. God knows what her trouble was. Perhaps she, too, was fatally in love.

Oh, the terrible, the irrevocable partings of childhood.

And these, of course, are only examples of the ordinary vicissitudes of life in a loving, sheltering family—no beatings, no shutting up in dark closets, the opposite of neglect and rejection—and therefore no explanation of anything.

I grew up, as I've said, in a pious churchgoing Methodist family; but in middle adolescence, almost without thinking about it, I lost interest in the church. What was said there no longer sounded sensible to me; the building seemed to crumble, the wind whistled through the gaps, and I moved out into the open desert. What I thought I was left with, even in the desert, was a conviction about human responsibility. One must cherish one's living, keep watch beside one's dying, bury one's dead. All answers could, must be worked out in relation to these necessities. But how? How?

And sexual infidelity? Clearly my own early affair should have prepared me for that. Honesty? Why should I care, here in the desert, whether George lies, whether my grandmother, his mother, our great-aunts and uncles, all, all lied?

And why do I continue frantically, like a Catholic at the hour of death, to confess?

Tuesday Oct. 28th

A young man who occasionally fills in as drummer in William's group reminds me very strongly of The Musk-rat. He has that curious sexual quality so repulsive to me in The M-r, a kind of quivering charge and with it a taint of prettiness, lips softly curved, ass too round, jeans too tightly stretched over the genitals. He's available—to anyone male or female who suits his always wavering fancy. Of course, that's what music, the kind he usually plays, is about. He's greatly in demand.

He doesn't precisely fit in William's group. Their music often makes an ironic, a comic comment on availability. And so, for William, he tries to send himself up. But the sexuality is so strong, no one believes his joke on himself. The camp followers come up afterwards, male and female, hysterical with lust. Here we are. Fuck us. Trample on us, kill us, whatever you like—we're yours.

This young man is twenty-eight or -nine, I suppose, looks eighteen or nineteen, still has to show his I.D. in a bar.

But why should the drummer's or The M-r's sexuality be repulsive to me? The lust of the goat is the glory of God.

Clearly, my friend—I'm talking to myself now—your age bears on this question. As soon as you asked yourself *Why?* a vision rose before your eyes of the old woman at the A&P, the old woman with the bile-yellow hair and rootlike muscles twisting under the bruised slack skin of her legs.

Oh, if I'm going to look like that, God, keep me out of the A&P. Let me be like Donatello's Magdalen instead, striding out, questing, the light of madness, of commitment in my eyes.

But George is no Jesus. He doesn't deserve me for a disciple.

Wednesday Oct. 29th

The Technician. Not The Musk-rat.

It's gross—inhuman—to call him by the name of an animal, to turn him into less than a man, to feel the rage and contempt that go into pronouncing, writing that word. And don't think I don't know when I do it who I am really calling an animal, making less than human. Again I think about calling him *The Technician*.

But that name, too, makes him less than the auburn-haired, dark-eyed lad, as lovely as Antinous, as human, as vulnerable to suffering as I.

Thursday Oct. 30th

Time passes. In conscientious pursuit of my policy of open-ness, I tell George in due course of my pain. Not to begin with. To begin with, the pain seems to me so irrational, so entirely contrary to what I sincerely believe I should be feeling that I say nothing. I wait for it to go away. But it doesn't go away.

He says again, "I'll give him up."

I say again, "No. No. That's not what I want."

He says, "For Christ's sake, what do you want?"

I cannot tell him what I want, although I know. To tell him would be self-defeating. For, of course, I want him not to want —that: the boy. And he has his desire no more under control than I my pain. I fear, too, that if I say, "Give him up," he will find some way to pretend he has. Lies again.

I say once more, "I want to want for you what you want for yourself. I want to care and let go.

"And I did, once, for a moment," I say. "I saw you look at him and smile and be happy and for one instant I was glad for your happiness, but the instant doesn't come back."

"Corinne, it has nothing to do with you. Do you see that? Nothing. What I feel for him has no connection with what I feel for you. If you could believe that . . ." He looked at me with his sad, ironic eyes. "I'm lonely—it's companionship that's most important to me. My friends— My friends, un-fortunately, are mostly dead. I need the friendship of a man."

But I didn't believe it. Not for a second.

I knew without doubt something else altogether, knew that for him to choose a man to lie down with . . . Ah, I can't even speak of it.

92

At some point, I forget when, I went a few times to see a psychotherapist. All my life I've been interested in psychiatric theory. I had read Havelock Ellis and Krafft-Ebing and Freud by the time I was twenty or so, then moved on to the others, Jung especially. I found him more to my taste than Freud, although the taint of Nazism was sinister. Later I read all the popularizations of this and that, from Menninger and Jones to Laing and Perls and Berne. But I had never tried it on myself, had managed by hook or by crook to hold my life together without taking to drink or flipping out.

Now— Now maybe I was flipping out. I went to a lady therapist. Again, as I had when I began again to fuck George, I went with passionate sincerity. I would go all the way—would follow my life into whatever abysses, whatever underground river, whatever culvert opening out into whatever sewage purification pond . . .

I told her everything I could think of to tell her. She was of the "acting out" school and we acted out all my hostilities toward George, toward my mother, my father, G.'s mother, etc.

Here again, age has its ludicrous side. At sixty-one I'm telling a total stranger sincerely, truthfully, how cold, how mean my mama was to me. Really! My poor maligned mother. Dead. Unable to defend herself.

I'm pounding a pillow and pretending it's George or the boy. Making up reasonable things they might say to me, plumping up the pillow, producing and addressing to it the horrid things I might say in reply.

I'm talking aloud to my "child," my hand, or the therapist's,

93

on my belly, as if we wait for her (the child) to give me a kick
—or perhaps knock out an answer in Morse code.

I had read with detached interest in the books on transac-
tional analysis of the three people occupying the crowded parlor of my soul: Parent, Child, and Adult; also, somewhat
smaller, but no less lively, several grandparents, who in their
turn influenced the Parent who holds my feet to the fire. Now,
I reasoned with my Child, reassured her, sang to her, told her
I would never, never abandon her, that I understood her rage
and anguish. I let her sob her little heart out. She became so
real to me I thought I might give birth to her. She was in there,
in my belly. Maybe if she popped out, she could take up her
separate abode in her own quarters. I thought of making her
a bed, like Kayo's in "Moon Mullens," in one of George's
bureau drawers. Let her torment him and leave me alone.

But that won't do. She's already tormenting him, telling him
about driving the car a hundred and twenty miles an hour,
about sitting on the floor of the can closet. What we need to
do is to make her happy and comfortable in there, so she won't
torment either one of us, so that she'll sleep, and wake only to
be playful, joyous, serene. In pursuit of this goal my therapist
held me in her arms and rocked me and comforted me. She
pretended she was George or Mama and let me beat on her.
We rolled on the floor together: She wore me out—she's quite
fit, runs two miles to work every day and plays a mean soccer
guard.

Perhaps it helped. Who knows? Who can tell? In any case
she was a tough cookie. I couldn't do that eight hours a day
for a living. My hat's off to her.

Friday Nov. 7th

I want to write now about going to California to see William.

But first, back in the jungle . . .

I went to see the boy. It was the day after he and George and I took in a movie together—the only time the three of us did anything together except occasionally exchange courteous greetings when I was on my way out of the house and he on his way in.

Yes, he did come to the house, to my house, some afternoons. Indeed, I suggested it. Why should G. not be able to do as he pleased in his own house? Hence my desire to chop up the bed.

Anyhow, the day after the movie I went to see him.

I was still floating around in the "I-want-to-want-for-you-what-you-want-for-yourself" soap bubble and I thought I might get to know him, to like him—never mind what names I called him—if we had a chance to talk to each other without George's embarrassing and stultifying presence between us. Oh, how generous-hearted, how saintly my intent!

Later

I sit here now, thinking, gazing out my window. The leaves are mostly down—all except for the great coppery mass of the chestnut oak in the curve of the levee and, on the beech trees, the clinging brown fans that will stay until spring. In winter, in the unmolested patch of woods between our house and the levee, once all the other leaves are down, one sees the bare gray trunks and limbs of pecans, the white bones of sycamores, the deep green splash of pine and cedar and smilax, and here and there a beech—still leafy, but brown, not green. I love the beech above all other trees, holding its warm leaves all winter, dropping them reluctantly when the sap begins to rise.

Perhaps taking a look at the woods has cleared my head. I will begin again. The fact is, it is hard for me to resist lying. I intended to invent a visit between me and the boy that would give you some insight into his miserable soul. He would say things to me that illustrated his selfishness, the coarseness of his sensibility, his stupidity, and I would report them without comment. Revenge! I was already concocting this revenge when I wrote early in October that I'd been to his house twice, that I'd confronted him alone.

But it never happened. I know nothing of his sensibility except . . .   But I'll come to that later. I never saw him alone. Never. Of course I didn't. How could I have gone to his house? Talked with him of our mutual interest in George? Even in my deluded passion to accept, accept, I would as soon have . . .

I, I, I was the one who thought of outrageous, coarse, stupid, selfish things that I might do or say to him, to them. How's a dash of Tabasco in the vaseline for starters?

But I know him only in my dreams, my fantasies. I could, for the purpose of this record, put our meeting in a dream, make him into a hostile or evil leading figure, and say the hateful things I wish to say, but in dreams, absurdly, the three of us are usually in bed together. Or perhaps we're examining feces together. I dream a lot about feces. Or . . .   See Sexual Appendix.

We did, truly, go to a movie together once in that early period. Sat on either side of good old George like children on either side of Daddy. It reminded me of going to church in my childhood, when my sister and I would sit on either side of my father, holding his hands, claiming him. Ugh.

And the movie was gloriously appropriate: *Close Encounters of the Third Kind*—a spiritual epiphany. One day we're all going to board a spaceship with some kindly spidery little men from another world, and then, finally—at last! to the accompaniment of mysterious music and the world's greatest light show, we'll understand what's going on in the universe.

Afterwards, stopping at Baskin-Robbins—he and George both like ice cream—he leaped out of the car as if he'd been goosed and ran in to get the cones while George and I enjoyed an interlude of light conversation. Oh, he (the boy) was unhappy that night, miserable. I remember his desperate smile as we drove him home, the two of them licking their cones, I holding mine, letting it melt and run down over my hand and my slacks. I remember his shifting eyes, his exaggerated courtesy. What else, poor bastard? He was poised already for flight.

And I did, truly, go to California to see William, spent a month with him.

Saturday Nov. 8th

Across the street from the modest house that William has bought high in the Montecito Hills of Los Angeles, overlooking a precipitous hillside that drops down to the Hollywood Freeway, live an elderly couple named Crouch who, after an initially suspicious period, have been very kind to him. To begin with, I feel sure, they had visions of all-night recording sessions blasting the neighborhood, of crazed drummers, high on cocaine, racing nude through the shrubbery. None of this happened and now they smile benevolently at William from their garden, even occasionally give him an avocado.

The husband used to be a Minister of Music in the Western Church of Redeemed Saints—of which, for all I know, they may be the founders—and she ran a day-care center for the children of the Redeemed, who must follow strict dietary laws based on the Mosaic Code and who believe that women will be excluded from heaven if they cut their hair, men if they spill their seed on the ground—or anywhere except in the Lord's appointed vessels, the insides of ladies—and that the bare feet of children should not touch the earth before puberty, lest their natural spirituality seep away before their skins become thickened and impervious to the suction exerted through the earth by the forces of evil.

Retired now, they spend their days building their lot. They scavenge the streets of the neighborhood—they seldom cross the freeway, because of the danger to their souls from diesel exhaust fumes—for limbs, grass clippings, broken chairs, rotten boards, discarded refrigerators, anything that doesn't stink and is maneuverable by two elderly people. The neighbors have gotten interested in their project, and in the case of something

98

as large as a refrigerator, the discarding owner will call and tell them about it and the young men in the neighborhood will help them to move it.

When they bought the house, it fronted on the street and its back end was propped on stilts above the steep hillside. They enclosed the space under the stilts and made a small basement, drove a row of pilings along a line ten feet out from the back wall, draped discarded rugs and propped planks against the pilings, and began to fill the area with trash. An occasional load of dirt scavenged from a foundation excavation went over the trash. In the rainy season they covered everything with Visqueen, punched holes in the covers, and planted squash vines, cucumbers, seedling fruit trees. After a couple of years they drove another row of pilings and began again. Now they have behind their house a blooming terraced garden that could be set down in the Umbrian hills. Avocado and lemon and orange trees overhang the stairs and pathways. Here is a terrace overgrown with squash vines, there a contour-plowed garden patch with tomatoes, green beans, eggplants. The roots of fig trees thrust downward to grip the old refrigerators and ovens and hold them in place. A small circular lawn juts out at the highest level, bordered by bougainvillea climbing on trellises and clipped hedges of jade. Here the Crouches sit in the evenings and survey their domain.

Below them, she tells me, she often sees coyotes, trotting the blasted weedy hillside. One bitch dens every year in a refrigerator that washed out from under the garden early in the project, before they mastered the technique of making land. She says she once saw the bitch bring home a small live dog for her pups to play with, bring down, and devour.

"I couldn't do anything about it," she says. "I can't get down there. I knew the Lord must have meant me to watch and I did. Everything has a purpose."

Why am I writing at such length about the Crouches? Perhaps because I made it a point on this visit to get acquainted with them. They distracted me from myself. And their confidence in William's respectability was valuable to him—he didn't want anybody calling the cops some night at four A.M. when the group was practicing and the keyboard man by chance left open the door of his soundproof studio. A mother—a sober, interested mother who asked the names of plants and gave out recipes for guava jelly was a prop not to be scorned.

And then later, as it turned out, for unforeseeable reasons, I spent considerable time in their garden.

I flew out to Los Angeles. Although by this time I was thinking of divorce, I had no intention, William, of discussing my predicament with you. How can one, without seeming to enlist support, to invite the choosing of sides? And now that I want to write of my visit, I am not addressing you, of course. You already know what happened with Janice Clifford and the Crouches and Janice's car and your house.

Sunday Nov. 9th

William began telling me what to expect as soon as we left the airport and set out on the forty-minute drive to his house. "I didn't say anything about it when you called," he said, "because I was afraid you'd back out if you knew. And you haven't been out here for over a year, after all—I wanted you to come."

I was busy looking at him. "You look great," I said, "although you know I like you better with a beard."

William is good-looking. (Doting mother speaks here.) Nice friendly brown eyes—friendly when they aren't bemused, listening to some melody make itself in his head—good profile, compact muscular body. I'm especially partial to his appearance when he has a beard. His hair is dark tawny blond and his beard is black as a pirate's. But beards are out now and short hair is in. He maintains what he considers an appropriate image for his group, as musicians have to do. He's an actor.

"What I need to tell you about is Janice Clifford."

"Who's Janice Clifford?"

She was renting a room in his house, he said.

William's house payments are steep for a struggling musician. Several months before my visit he had parted traumatically from the woman he'd lived with for four years, who had shared expenses with him; and just as he'd made up his mind that he would have to rent a room to make ends meet, Janice had called him. He'd known her when he lived in Nashville early in his musical career. She was a classical violist who had decided she would never make it in the music world, had gone back to school, and got a degree in computers. She had recently left her husband and come out to Los Angeles to a new job.

"She's in the guest room," he said. "I've fixed up my bedroom for you and put a rollaway bed in the studio for me." He had soundproofed his third bedroom and turned it into a studio and rehearsal room.

I studied his profile as he maneuvered the car through rush-hour traffic on the Santa Monica Freeway. There was something he had not said.

He glanced at me. "OK?"

"Is this a sexual arrangement?"

He shook his head, laughed ruefully. "Hardly."

"Just curious. I'm glad you have somebody you know. Just hope she stays."

"Maybe. Maybe not," he said. "She's getting out of hand. I don't know what to do about her."

Janice, he had discovered after she was settled in his house, had come to L.A. for a specific reason. She was in love with Eugene Fodor.

"Who?"

"You know. The violinist everybody—I mean everybody in classical music circles, not in my circles—is so crazy over. You've seen his picture in *Time*, haven't you? He's a beautiful guy. And she's in love with him. Has his pictures plastered all over her room."

"Where'd she get to know him? Juilliard?"

"No, no. That's the problem. She doesn't know him. She saw him on the Johnny Carson show.

"I suppose it's partly my fault I didn't notice anything unusual about her," he said. "The music has been going well lately and I haven't thought about anything else. I've written ten new songs this month, Mama. Warner's is looking at a couple of them."

"That's great," I said.

"Yes, it's great if anything happens. You know how that goes." He pulled into an exit road, started the climb toward his house. "But Janice. She didn't tell me to begin with . . . She's nutty on the subject of this man."

She had seen him on the tube, William said. He'd looked straight into her eyes, spoken to her alone, told her he was going to Los Angeles to perform, to visit friends, perhaps to stay for some months. She had known she must follow him. Without a word to anyone she went—left her husband and baby and the job she was scheduled to go back to at the end of her maternity leave and boarded the first plane to L.A.

"Everything was straight until she got moved in," he said. "She was getting a divorce, that was all. I like her. She was nervous, I saw that. She wandered the house at night . . . But she wanted to get along. She'd go to Watts or someplace where you can buy mustard greens in the supermarkets, bring everything back, and cook up a big Southern supper. You know how I love greens and corn bread. And she had an absolutely bottomless supply of dope. I don't smoke much any more, but she was always offering it, always cooking up something.

"And then she began to talk about him. Now she talks about him more and more, says he needs her, spends hours on the weekends driving the freeways, thinking she'll see him. It's just a matter of time, she says. She's smoking more (although who knows, she may always have been stoned). She has a good job with the city and she does get herself up in the morning, goes to work, pays the rent. But a couple of times at night I've come out of the studio and found her out cold on the living room floor, the saucepan with the greens in it on the stove, the stove going full blast, the pot burned up . . . Did you know you can break one of those old black iron skillets? You remember you gave me one when I went to Nashville? She left it on the fire until it was red—glowing—and then put it under the faucet. Burned her hand, too, although she had a potholder. The skillet broke right in two." Again he glanced sheepishly at me. "So that's what you're getting into," he said. He laughed. "I don't have any suacepans left and damned if I'll buy some more for her to burn up. Besides, I don't have time. I don't have time for anything now."

"Why don't you tell her she has to move?"

"I feel sorry for her, Mama. She's not . . . responsible. Besides . . ." He broke off, but I knew what "besides" meant in William's terms. He has a passivity in his character, an almost Oriental belief in the inevitability, the value of everything that happens to him. And he's always attracted, tolerated, been screwed by strays.

He began again. "She gave me a song. How can I kick her out of my house when she's given me a song?" He hummed a frenetic, driving tune and then sang a yearning, contrasting, drawn-out chorus: " 'You can be/ whatever you want—to—be/ If you can/ Leave—the—world—behind.' "

"Are you afraid she might kill herself? Or what?"

"I don't know. Anything's possible. She's crazy, Mama."

"What about family? Her husband?"

He shook his head. "She's twenty-nine years old. I can't tell her what to do, who to call."

"The baby," I said. "She left her baby? How old is it?"

"The baby's new," he said, "just a couple of months old when she left."

"Maybe it's a postpartum psychosis. Even more important to get hold of somebody responsible. What about her parents?"

"What I was getting ready to tell you—the day after she saw him—Fodor—on the tube, she bundled up the baby, put him in a plastic laundry basket, called a taxi, and on her way to the airport, stopped, left him on her parents' doorstep, rang the doorbell, got back in the cab, and continued on her way. She didn't want to have to go through a scene, she said."

"Jesus Christ, William!"

"I didn't know any of this until last week. She told all the night she burned up the skillet and blistered her hand."

"Does her family know where she is?"

"What she told me was that her husband has no interest in the child, didn't want it in the first place, and won't be responsible for it. Her parents— Yes, they know she's here. She says they don't care, don't want her to come home or to have the child or interfere with their care of it. It's that kind of thing.

She's been a lost soul, I suppose, for a long time . . . It's not new, not postpartum."

"What are you going to do about her?" I said.

"She gave me a song," he repeated. Abruptly he shifted ground. "She's gotten chummy with the Crouches," he said. "She can watch the freeway from one of their lower terraces and she's bought a pair of binoculars. That's what she does on weekends and in the late afternoons. Mrs. Crouch is trying to convert her to Redeemed Saints. That would be as good a thing as any . . ."

"Watch the freeway?"

"She thinks he's going to ride by. Hell, Mama, I don't know. Anyway, when she's over there, she's out of my hair."

Monday Nov. 10th

I suppose all my latent motherly passions must have been aroused by William's account of their predicament—toward William, who needed peace and quiet for his work—not to mention a new set of pots and pans, toward the miserable woman in the grip of her obsession, toward the abandoned baby. I get to mother my grandchildren, of course, I feel again the familiar stir, the drawing down behind the nipple of ghostly milk. But here was material for more complex maternal talents.

Janice and I spent considerable time together in the evenings while William was working; and her gentleness, her childlike trust touched me. She was passionate, but convincing —consistent—in her love for Mr. Fodor. She talked about his music, about her own abandoned talent, about the way his sound went straight to her gut, about how musicians need nurturing, sheltering from their fans—particularly if, like him, they're handsome, personable, have been seized on for the moment by the talk shows, the celebrity makers.

She took me to her room the first time we talked. It was the neat, bookish retreat of a student, smelling faintly and sweetly of marijuana. Her viola lay on top of a chest. A small improvised bookcase of planks and bricks held a potted bromeliad, a row of paperbacks, a stack of sheet music, a cassette player, and cassettes. The only unusual thing about it was what she had brought me in to see: three large posters of him—handsome, boyish, his lids borne down by heavy lashes, his lips sensitive and sorrowful, looking with passionate concentration at his violin.

"He's the prisoner of his gift," she said.

I agreed that quite possibly he was.

She sat down on the bed, leaned against the headboard, motioned me to a chair, and continued to gaze at him, one long leg bent at the knee, the other stretched out, twitching steadily at the ankle. She was an attractive-looking woman—tall and slender with a high round forehead and curly dark hair. I noticed particularly her skin, white and opaque and fine-pored, as if it were a layer thicker than ordinary skin. She had light blue eyes, and when she stopped looking at him and looked at me, I saw in them, too, a kind of poreless opacity. Her nose was straight and delicately modeled, her upper lip a trifle short, so that she seemed, always, even when she was smiling, to be sniffing the air for something she had not yet identified.

On Saturday when William had closed himself in the studio with his group, she took me down to one of the lower terraces of the Crouches' garden.

". . . literally the prisoner of his career," she went on from two days before, as if we were continuing a conversation that played itself over and over in her head. "Agents, business managers—*trolls*—everyone conspires to keep him away from the people he needs to nurture him, the ones who would understand him . . ." Attentively she watched the faraway freeway through her binoculars, talking all the while. "That night," she said, "I saw it all in an instant. When numbskull Johnny Carson in his wide silk tie and his foxy jacket and foxy smile, when he asked Eugene a question, I saw an expression cross his face—Eugene's—indescribable, as if he retreated into some deep place inside himself. I knew and he knew—he would know, if only he had a chance to—that I was the only one who belonged there." She sighed and shook her head, sniffed the air, and put aside the binoculars to gaze at me out of poreless eyes.

She explained that afternoon that she had seen a car on the freeway in which she believed he was riding—surrounded by hangers-on. "They're animals—wolves, coyotes, vultures." She caught a glimpse of his face, got the first three digits of the license plate, but couldn't be sure.

"Isn't he married, Janice?" I asked abruptly.

She drew back as if I'd slapped her, stood up, turned away. "She's as bad as the rest of them. I know." She took up her binoculars, ignored me for a long time, then began to talk again, as if we'd never mentioned his wife.

She explained that this freeway was one he would have to take from the home of his friend in Santa Monica to the recording studios where he would be working. She had studied the city map and questioned William about the location of studios, the neighborhoods where rich artists live. "He *will* pass," she said.

"Perhaps he's gone," I said.

"If he left, there would be a big story in the *Times*," she said. "I know what his concert dates are this year. He hasn't gone."

She seemed so reasonable, so gentle. I was sure I could help her abandon this obsession.

She looked straight at me more than once and said, "I know it's hopeless, ridiculous, but I can't help myself."

Lots of crazy people, as anyone who deals with them knows, are not crazy.

"If you know," I said, "maybe you can help yourself. We'll help you to help yourself."

The will to action and the act are everything. But then, on the other hand, does the will even exist?

"I see strange things on the freeway," she told me that afternoon. She handed me the binoculars and pointed out a pedestrian crossover that, unlike most, was not shielded with wire netting against suicides and murderers. "I see people walk across," she said. "I see them stop. I wonder if they're looking for someone, waiting for someone, to pass below them. Sometimes I see in their faces a terrible grief. I wonder if they are so sad they're thinking of jumping down into the rush-hour traffic. People do that, of course. Or are they full of ecstasy? Do they think, if they jump, they might fly up over the freeway on the updraft like human hang gliders?"

"You can be whatever you want to be/ If you can leave the world behind . . ."

Mrs. Crouch had come onto the terrace above us. "Those poor people, the cells of their spiritual bodies have been captured by diesel fumes," she said. "Their spirituality has been paralyzed."

Mrs. Crouch, who was originally trained as a dental hygienist, had explained to me that the corporeal body and the spiritual body occupy the same space; that the immense so-called "empty" space between the nucleus of an atom and its electron shell is, in the case of each atom of a human body, occupied by a twin atom of spirituality, that the most potent danger to spirituality is from diesel exhaust fumes, which "freeze" these spiritual atoms in their physical shells and para-lyze the spiritual life of the individual. Up here on the hilltop, where the diesel trucks never come, we are safe from the fumes, she says, but one must avoid the freeways whenever possible and, if one has to use them, must prepare for these excursions with strengthening prayers. We have all read, she says, of the wasp that paralyzes a caterpillar and then lays in its flesh an egg that will hatch and eat the caterpillar alive. In the same way we can go on living, even though we are spiritually paralyzed, and furnish food for the larvae of evil, the children of the devil.

"One day," Janice said, "I saw a woman walk across, holding two little children by their hands. They stopped for a long time in the middle of the walkway. I thought maybe the woman's husband had abandoned her, that she was watching the free-way as I do, knowing that his car would eventually pass, that she would find out where he was going and . . ."

"Were the children barefooted?" Mrs. Crouch asked. "Oh, no one knows how important it is to keep shoes on children in their formative years. The soles of the feet are *vulnerable*."

"I see you looking at me," Janice said to me, "and I know you're thinking that I left my husband, abandoned my baby. But I didn't. I knew that I could only contaminate the child with my obsessions, that he would be better off without me, that, who knows, I might destroy him. When I have everything worked out . . ."

"She's going to go back and get him when she gets her problems straightened out, aren't you, dear?" Mrs. Crouch said. "I'm going to help her with him."

Mrs. Crouch took hold of her wheelbarrow full of bagged grass clippings, guided it down a long curving ramp at one end of her domain, and emptied the bags into an area contained by a new row of pilings. Her thin, crinkled tissue-paper skin was dry even in the August heat, her black eyes bright with calculation as she poured each bag into the precise spot that needed mulching. She tramped back up the ramp in her sensible nurses' shoes, dragging the wheelbarrow behind her. Her figure was squat and strong from years of building, a hump of fat like a camel's rising between her shoulders. Now she looked down at us with a calculation, an attention as fierce as that she had given the grass. "I'd like for you to come to church with me and Crouch, my dears," she said. "I know you can find answers there . . ." She did not wait for either of us to speak, but set out for the street. "The Calloways have put out some lovely trash," she called back to us.

"I've thought of exactly what I want to do for him," Janice said. "A gift I can make for him. And I know when I give it to him, when he sees how much he means to me, he'll open his heart . . ."

"You're talking foolishness, you know," I said. "You know that. Let us help you find someone to advise you, someone to help you get rid of this obsession. We're concerned about you."

"My car," Janice said. "There'll be a meaning in that for him that only he and I will understand. I can do that for him and . . ." She had taken back her binoculars and was watching the freeway again.

"Are you listening to me, Janice?"

"Do you mean you think I should see a psychiatrist? If you think that would do me any good, you need to see a psychiatrist yourself. Do you know how many I've seen in the last fifteen years? Of course there's no way you could, but I lost count a long time ago. I drift from life to life and in every life somebody says, 'My dear, you need to see a psychiatrist.' I've *seen* them. But here's a twist, a sensible question: Has a psychiatrist ever seen me?"

"Of course there are quacks," I said. "And there are limited people in psychiatry just as . . ."

"Ridiculous people," Janice said. "They think it's possible to be sane. That they—they!—can explain things."

"There are drugs that might help you," I said firmly.

"I've thought of exactly what I want to do for him," Janice said. "A gift I can make for him. And I know— It's my car. There'll be a meaning in it for him that only he will understand. I can do that for him and . . ."

"What are you talking about?"

"Do you know what it's like to fall in love?" She was still watching the freeway as she talked. "It's like having been buried for years, like being an ant lion, a doodlebug, and then one day you crawl out of your skin and your wings unfold and you're a new creature—a locust, a katydid."

"Yes," I said. "It's like that."

"You're a very sensitive person, if you *are* sixty years old," she said.

I gave her a look, but said nothing.

She stretched out her arms toward the freeway. "Oh, if he knew me," she said. "If only he knew me." Mrs. Crouch was clattering up the driveway with her cart again. "Fred and Wanda have thrown away the most marvelous rug pad," she said. "Exactly what I need to anchor the west end of the low terrace." And then, "Look, my dears! Look! There she goes. Look quickly!"

We walked to the edge of the terrace in time to see Mrs. Crouch's coyote trotting along the slope a hundred yards below the garden, her head held high, her teeth gripping a small, struggling body—what appeared to be a puppy. Perhaps it was a large rat.

"What's the message here?" Mrs. Crouch said in a low and wondering voice. "What is He telling me?"

Why am I writing this account of Janice Clifford's obsessions, Mrs. Crouch's obsessions, that seems to have nothing to do with my predicament? Surely you see, my dears, that I saw myself in that miserable girl—that it came to seem to me sometimes that George was as much a figment of my imagination as Eugene Fodor was of hers, that I feared I might find myself one day watching some distant freeway with binoculars, waiting for George and the boy to drive by. And probably, too, with all this elaboration of other people's lives, I am putting off getting to the way my own obsessions, my own dreams did finally seize me by the throat and shake me until I felt my bones split.

Be patient. Let me go on.

Tuesday Nov. 11th

Two weeks went by. Janice thought of nothing but the decoration of her car. She spent hours making sketches. She explained to William, as she had to me, that she intended to give the car, once she had finished decorating it, to *him*. "It will be uniquely beautiful," she said.

"How will you get to work?" William said.

"Maybe you could lend me your car some days and I could get into a pool other days."

"Janice," he said reasonably, "you know I can't do that. I have to have my car."

"It wouldn't hurt me to walk," she said. "All the time I was walking, I could be thinking of him riding in my car, the most beautiful car in Los Angeles. And I would probably see him. I couldn't miss him."

"Janice!"

Work was not so far for Janice as it is for some Angelenos —just a mile or so down the hill to the freeway and then only seven or eight to the exit closest to the complex of municipal buildings that house her computer bank.

"William, it won't be long before I can afford to make a down payment on another car—just a couple of paychecks. I can work something out until then."

She got up, went to her room, and came out shortly with her sketch pad and pens and brushes. "I'm going over to the garden to sketch," she said. At the door she paused, sniffed the air as if she might identify some faint trace of poison. "I'm getting to the place where I don't know whether or not I can trust you, William," she said. "You may be a part of the screen. You and your mother, too. All you do is put obstacles in my way."

In the garden, binoculars by her side, she worked over her sketch pad for hours. She intended to choose leaves of suitably varying shapes and sizes and glue them in designs all over her car, to connect the leaves with wandering musical staves, to work out the leaf veins with strings of notes, themes from works he liked best to play and from those she cared most for. Long fern fronds would curl over the fenders, tendrils of wandering Jew would drop down from the roof and frame the side and rear windows. There would be a philodendron gigantica leaf on either front door. By evening she had forgotten her suspicions of us and showed us the finished design, with elevations from every angle.

"Once it's all put together," she said, "I'll spray the car with clear acrylic."

"Don't you think the leaves may shrivel and lose their color?" I said.

"Not if I seal them properly."

Later on that week she saw him on a local talk show. His appearance had, of course, been announced in the L.A. *Times* television schedule.

Again, it appeared, he spoke only to her.

That night she telephoned a friend of Fodor's whom he had mentioned in the course of the interview—a musician who lived in New York. He would be able to get word through about the car, tell her when and where to deliver it. She became agitated when this man refused to help her.

"If I were in New York, I would kill him," she said matter-of-factly to William. "He's another of those sycophants, those snakes, worms, boa constrictors who keep Eugene away from his true friends. From me. When he needs me, wants me. Or he would, if I could get to him—if I could only get to him."

That night, after she had gone to her room and closed the door and turned on her cassette player to listen again to one of his records, William called her parents.

Afterwards he told me about the other end of the conversation.

Mrs. Clifford answered the telephone, listened to him identify himself and then without a word left the telephone and shouted for her husband. After a long silence he came to the phone and answered. Then William heard the click of another receiver being taken off the hook.

Mr. Clifford listened to William's description of Janice's condition. Then: "If you don't want her in your house," he said, "tell her to leave. You have the choice. It's your problem. It's as simple as that."

William's voice grew gentler. "Sir," he said—he's a Southern boy and knows the value of a deferential *sir*—"of course it *is* my problem. You're right. But . . ."

"If you could know the humiliation she's caused us," her father said. "The embarrassment. Her sisters are ashamed to admit they're related to her. And now this— This illegitimate . . . this bastard child. I suppose she told you she was married. But it's a bastard in the eyes of God. Some fly-by-night j.p. married them, *if* they're married at all. And now he's taken up with another woman and gone off, God knows where." He grunted with disgust. "But we do our duty by the child," he said. "And she can be sure she'll never get it back from us. Tell her that. As to what *your* duty is— Are you married? Where's your wife? Are you taking advantage of her condition? You're bound to know her brains have been burned up with all that marijuana. Are you . . . using her?"

"Sir, she's renting a room from me," William said.

"What does that mean? That could mean anything."

"I'm afraid she may hurt herself." As the conversation continued, his voice grew gentler and gentler. "Or someone else. I think she's not responsible for what she does. She won't see a psychiatrist."

"The money we've spent on psychiatrists," he said.

"Someone who has the right to be responsible for her needs to . . ."

"I know how hard it is to evict renters," he said. "We're all tied hand and foot by the federal government. You'll just have to do the best you can."

Throughout, William heard the mother breathing, but she never spoke.

As it turned out, Janice brought an end to—I was about to say an end to our difficulties, but that wouldn't be strictly true. She left, but not without producing a new set of difficulties for William. And God knows where her difficulties will end.

Two nights later, after another attempt to get her to a psychiatrist—William had found one and arranged the appointment, but she had refused to go—he and I went out for dinner and a movie. By this time we could hardly bear to mention her to each other, but on the way home he said, "I've got to put a stop to it, Mama. I'm going to rent a room for her at a motel tomorrow and take her things down to it."

We did not look at each other.

"Christ, what else can I do?" he said. "I've got to live, too."

"I know," I said.

We drove up the steep, winding road toward his house, heard before we got there the sound of sirens, looked at each other.

"It's my block," he said. And then: "Shit, Mama, it's my house."

We found the house in flames, two fire engines in front, fire spurting through the roof above the bedroom where I had been sleeping.

"Jesus Christ!" he said. "Janice! Where's Janice?" He was out of the car before it rolled to a stop, a neighborhood child running along beside us, his hand on the window, shouting, "It's your house, William. Your house is on fire." He stumbled over hoses, pushed his way through the gathered neighbors, grabbed the first fireman he came to. "There was a woman in there," he said. "She may have been sleeping. Did you get her out?"

"Who are you?"

"A woman! Did you hear me? I live here."

"Yeah, one of the neighbors got her out. She's over there." He jerked his thumb toward the Crouches' house. "They took her home with them. She wasn't hurt."

"My tapes," he said. "My songs. The console." He started toward the fire like a sleepwalker. Flames leaped toward him through the kitchen door. The fireman pulled him back.

How was it after that? We stood with our arms about each other. I wept. "It's all right, Mama," he said. "It's all right. I can put them together again. Everything's in my head. Everything."

What sticks with me is living ten days in the sooty blackness of the burned-out shell. He would not leave and we made do in the undamaged bedroom and bath, carrying lamps on extension cords around the house, gazing into empty, sooty caverns, making insurance lists, boarding up windows; picking through the rubble and the piles of wet sawdust for tapes, cassettes, scraps of music manuscript, and business records; finding a piece of the leather coat we'd given him for Christmas four years ago, a corner of a rug, charred fragments of a table, the ruin of a mattress; going to Sears to buy clothes and weeping again among the racks of polyester pants suits.

We did not see her. She hid herself in the Crouches' house, did not come out. We inquired for her, of course.

"We take this as a direct sign from God," Mrs. Crouch said the next day. "She's converted, put that old life behind her. Hasn't a thread left out of it. We're following an intensive study program—we've already started. It's wonderful. She knows God saved her for a purpose."

William was genuinely interested. I suppose he was hoping he'd get another song. He tried to clean himself up—you couldn't touch a light switch or a doorknob without getting sooty—and went to call. But Mrs. Crouch wouldn't let him in.

"I'd like to talk to her about the fire," he said.

"She's already told the people from the fire department everything she knows and that's not much. She was asleep when it started. If I hadn't been outside picking up a few bags of clippings over at Fred's, if I hadn't heard that sound like rushing water, like a flood—God's signal—but it was the rushing of flame, she'd never have gotten out. Never!"

"But . . ." The fire had started in the kitchen, of course. She must have left a burner on under a pan.

"She's in a very nervous state, William. Maybe in a few days . . . The important thing now is not to do anything that will disturb her spiritual structures."

"What about . . . ?"

"She's given up all that foolishness about the musician and decorating the car," Mrs. Crouch said. "She sees it was God giving her a message about that with the fire. Her design and her sketchbook and all burnt up, didn't it? She's put herself in my hands. And it's just a matter of time until we get that baby of hers and get some shoes on him."

There was a message in it for William, too, as it turned out. He had excellent insurance and it paid off. He did most of the work on the house himself with the help of a couple of unemployed musicians who were also carpenters. My sons can turn their hands to almost anything—Corinne can, too, for that matter. He saved at least half the insurance money and that put him in a position to coast for a few months, slack off on performing, and get some new songs written.

I left the following Sunday and flew home in William's khakis and T-shirt, carrying an overnight bag that had survived the fire, though it was dampish and smelled like burnt toast.

That morning, before he took me to the airport, while I sat in William's small side yard drinking instant coffee and eating a grapefruit off his tree and looking at the morning paper, I heard a commotion across the street in the Crouch household. A door slammed. I was weary, didn't want to see any more of those maniacs. I drew my chair behind a thicket of straggling smoke-shrouded jade plants. Through the foliage I saw Janice running down the front steps and around the corner of the house toward the terraced garden. She was wearing a house-dress of Mrs. Crouch's, a faded print garment that stopped short of her knees and enveloped the upper part of her long slender body like a poncho; her binoculars were slung over her shoulder. Had she been wearing them when she fell asleep the night of the fire? If not, she must have snatched them up on her way out of the house. Another door slammed. I heard voices, hers and Mrs. Crouch's, an unintelligible argument. Then shouts again.

Janice: "I know. I know, for Christ's sake."

Mrs. Crouch: "Just give them to me. And do not take the name of the Lord in vain."

Janice ran back around the house, dress flapping against her thighs, stepped down into the street, holding the binoculars in her hand, lifted them to her eyes, turning, sweeping the length of the street to her left and then to her right, raised them and looked eastward above the scorched tops of the palm trees, straight, as it seemed to me, into the morning sun. "Oh, ohhh," she said, not loud, meditatively, and then, louder, calling, "Where *are* you?"

William must have heard the uproar, for he stepped out of the house now, started toward her. "Janice," he said. "Janice? Can't we . . . ?" He reached out. "Come on over," he said, "any time you need to."

But she backed away. "What am I doing here," she said, "in this street, this life?"

I wrapped my arms around my breasts, dug my nails into my rib cage to keep from weeping.

Mrs. Crouch made her way along the driveway, weighed down by her camel's hump of fat, and stood watching. "Give them to me, my dear," she said again. She stepped into the street and laid her hand on Janice's shoulder, but Janice jerked free, turned away, strode off down the block.

"You're morally responsible for every step you take," Mrs. Crouch shouted after her. "Just remember that, will you? Morally responsible."

At the airport, in the tickets-already-purchased check-in line, William looked at me with George's sad ironic eyes and kissed me tenderly. "It's all right, Mama," he said. "Don't be sad."

As he walked away, he was whistling a new tune. I recognized it because he had already picked it out on the piano for me and sung the refrain: "A fire is on the land . . ." It was about a much more general conflagration than his, of course, but he said that the thought, that night as he jumped from the moving car, that Janice might be inside, and then the heat, like a blow, that had thrown him back from the kitchen door, the charred and melted remnants of his music, had got him started thinking about disaster.

Wednesday Nov. 12th

Not many weeks after I got back from California, he—The M-r—broke off his affair with George and moved away from our city.

George had known it must come, had once said to me, "It can't last, Corinne. I know he'll leave me."

I, on my side, had doggedly repeated to myself over and over (for how long? a year?), he'll wake up. He'll see how impossible this creature is. He'll come back to me.

To George I had said, "Go away with him, for Christ's sake. Live with him. That's what you need to do. Decide if you want to commit yourself to him for life."

I'd said it when I was half crazy, but I'd meant it.

But he had looked at me in wonder: "My God, Corinne, I love you!" and then added: "Besides, he doesn't want that."

Shit!

Understand that even though I wrote "creature," I am trying to say as little as possible about my version of him and about what George said of him. I could, after all, scarcely fail to distort—if not deliberately, then inadvertently. But I feel my hatred of him pounding against my diaphragm like waves, piercing my throat like needles of rain in a tornado.

I think again about The Toad and her church. I may have fabricated that drama to suggest that the boy is contemptible for his hypocrisy. Have you thought of that? I must have wanted that scene to attach itself to him without your realizing that it had done so.

That he married that miserable born-again woman because she "kept him in line," as George said, speaks for itself, doesn't it?

Enough. I don't know anything about that, not anything. In any case, he left.

He was bitterly unhappy with his homosexual life, George said. He wanted to be straight, to project some reasonably normal image of himself (jargon, all jargon) into the lives of his children. He had decided that a new scene where no one would know anything about him, where he would not be subject to all the temptations of the gay scene here, would be better for him.

"He's deluding himself," George said. "He can't live without it. He has to have a man."

I listened in silence, thinking various things.

It occurred to me, for example, that George might be doing the projecting—projecting the intensity of his own feelings onto the boy. It was George who could not live without *it*, without him.

I thought also that there was a gay scene everywhere, that there were many potential lovers in the world for The Muskrat, male and female, unencumbered by crazy wives who made you miserable by "accepting" your "relationship" with their husbands.

I thought that George was fifty-nine, the boy twenty-seven, the world all before him.

As for Geroge, he was—what?

If I used a word like "inconsolable," it would sound as if I meant to be ironic—to suggest that his predicament was somehow comic. I mean no such thing. Irony had no part in my feelings—except perhaps toward myself. I did, indeed, even when I was suffering most intensely, think of my own predicament as to a degree comic. But George?

I thought he might kill himself.

If, to begin with, he had fled death to the boy's arms, now he would as soon be dead as be without him. It was as if the boy were youth itself, had taken away with him when he went the intermittently shocking current, the pacemaker that kept G.'s heart beating. To keep himself alive now he had only work.

He took on another shift at the hospital, regularly worked a seventy-two-hour week. He volunteered for shifts whenever one of the younger men wanted to be off. At home he read no poetry, recited no poetry, read nothing. He doggedly turned and turned his vegetable garden, fell asleep from exhaustion. I would wake in the night, uneasily aware of some difference in his breathing, to realize that he was lying beside me wide awake, rigid, silent, waiting for the relief of a new day's work. In the morning he would rise silently to labor again—out in his garden at seven, gone to the hospital by noon even on the days when he was supposed to check in at three.

It was early spring now, time to put in spinach, lettuce, broccoli, mustard greens. But he had not yet planted anything. He had borrowed a pickup, brought home manure and lime, carted his compost heap across the yard and dumped it on the lime, turned and turned and turned the earth, rowed it up, decided he wanted the rows to run the other way, reworked and redesigned the plot, made an elaborate new asparagus bed, prepared the ground for strawberries, but planted nothing.

I was standing watching him before I left for class one day, silent, as we had been with each other now for weeks. "Don't you think you'd better plant the spinach?" I said. "If you don't, we won't get any before the hot weather kills it."

"It would be better if I were dead," he said. "I'd be better off. You'd be better off. I think about it. But I'm a coward." He went on thrusting the spade into the ground, turning and breaking it, spadeful by spadeful.

I felt as I might if a giant struck me a blow on the heart with his clenched fist. How deeply he must hate me, then! Far more deeply than I had dreamed. I looked at him for a long time.

"What's your purpose in saying that to me?" I said. "Are you trying to blackmail me? Into what? He's the one to try your blackmail on."

"I'm telling you how I feel. You've said from the beginning that the only good thing about all this is that we can be honest with each other, know each other. I'm telling you what I feel."

"No," I said. "After all, it isn't blackmail. There's nothing you want from me. It's just a statement of what you feel to be the value of our life together. You'd rather be dead than living here with me."

"What I'm saying, Corinne, is that it would be the best thing for you. You could at least go about making a life for yourself."

"If you want to die, that's your choice," I said. "There's nothing I can do about it. But don't think you can get away with putting it off on your concern for me. That's the laugh of the century."

"I just want to be dead," he said. "That's all. I want to be dead."

And then he wept and I wept, and I comforted him there in the backyard under the cold March sky, took his head on my breast, as I had longed to do that day so many years ago when he had mourned his dead patient. I held him and comforted him at last, not for the loss of his patient, but for the loss of his young lover, whom he so passionately wanted to be leaning against him, lying beside him in my place.

Tuesday Nov. 18th

George would not, could not let him go. He called him long distance again and again, spoke of the loss of friendship (or told me that was what he spoke of), persuaded him that they should "keep up" with each other. The loss of friendship was the important thing, he said. Friendship, so much rarer, so much more precious, after all, than . . .

They began to exchange letters. They wrote each other weekly. They would be friends.

Before long George arranged to attend a medical meeting in the city to which the boy had moved. I knew when he came back that the affair had started up again. One look at his face: I didn't think or suspect; I knew. As if to bear me out, he began to read poetry, to recite through his shaving cream in the morning—" 'When such as I cast our remorse . . .' "—whistle as he set off for work. After a couple of months he dropped the third shift he had taken on at the hospital.

What he said, however, was that the affair was over—absolutely over.

"It doesn't matter what I want," he said. "I have no say in the matter. He says, 'No.' "

He did not omit, you see, to strike me on the heart with his fist. Again, when I looked at him, he said, "I'm trying to be honest. You've said you want me to be honest."

By now I knew how hopeless it was for me to struggle with my jealousy. I knew I was a failure. Pitiful creature that I am, I could not love him, I could love only my dream of him, my own obsession.

Oh, is there no way, no way at all to purge ourselves of our madness, to be nobler than we are?

But more important even than this mean, humiliating self-knowledge was something else that happened as soon as George and The M-r began to correspond and to see each other again. (He would come back for a weekend to visit his former housemates and to see his children, or George would find a professional reason to go to his city.)

I knew it was happening—I tried, I did, to prevent it. I felt the north wind of madness stripping away the last shred of my dignity, the last worn garment of my pride, penetrating, freezing the brittle aging bone of my honor, making of me such a creature as you might see in a dime store stealing—not bread for her children, but worthless trinkets.

I tried to "save myself" by telling George what was in my mind.

I said: "I know you're fucking him again. My attention all my life, my professional attention, has been on people's faces and on the relationship between what they say and what they mean. If it weren't, I couldn't survive in the teaching profession. So I know."

I said: "Please tell me the truth. I know you love me. We can manage if only . . ."

I said: "I have the right to know the terms of my own life. To decide how I want to live—whether I can handle this or whether it would be better to leave. Haven't I? Haven't I?"

"Yes," he said. "That's true." Then he said, "Corinne, you have friends, you know—friends you care about who aren't necessarily my friends. That's all it is now. I've told you that. You can forget the other."

"You've gone back into the love affair," I said.

"What difference does it make what I say to you? Will it satisfy you if I say *yes,* even though I'd be lying?"

I said, "I've lived with you thirty years. If my perception of you is false, then I perceive nothing truly. I'm insane. If I'm insane, I need to know it."

(How can you "know" you're crazy? I didn't proceed that far with my reasoning, because I knew I wasn't crazy as confidently as I knew I was.)

I would tell you where we were, what was going on while we had this conversation, what was significant in our gestures and our appearance; but we had it more than once. We had it in the garden while he put in tomato plants and pulled a fresh layer of dirt over his asparagus roots. We had it in the living room, where he laid down his paper, folded his arms across his chest, and drew in his leg. We had it when my hair was wild and blowing in the wind and my face swollen with weeping, my legs bruised from running into tables in the dark; and when I was dressed in my best wool slacks and silk shirt and tweed jacket, headed for a symposium on the modern novel; and when he came out of the bedroom in the middle of the night and joined me in the kitchen, where I sat staring at the ghosts in the television set.

"Listen to me, George. I am falling to pieces. I want to tell you what is in my mind, so you'll understand how desperate my situation is. I know you keep his letters. You keep them in your pocket until I'm not here and then you hide them someplace. They're in this house. I want you to know that I'm tempted. They come, and first I am tempted to steam them open or to take one, just take it and never give it to you. After I don't do that, I'm tempted to look through the house until I find them, wherever you have hidden them."

All the time I was talking, he was shaking his head. "Corinne," gently, his voice like William's when he was talking to Janice's father, "if I wanted to hide something in our friendship from you, all I would have to do would be to tell him to send his letters to the hospital instead of here."

"Where any receptionist, any secretary in Receiving might open them?"

He kept shaking his head.

"I think if I open one of his letters, I mean if I read it, even if he says nothing significant, even if it's about the weather, I'll know; and I'll know whether or not I'm crazy. I can't leave you for a cause that exists only in my head. I love you."

"I love you," he said.

"So I have to find them. I warn you now, if I find them, I

may read them. I *will* read them. I'm telling you to save myself from that."

"Corinne, you're not being reasonable. For Christ's sake, I could rent a post office box. Besides, the fact is, I don't keep them. You know very well I never keep letters. I keep them until I answer them, and then I tear them up. That's all there is to it."

I said, "It's not that I want to read what he says to you. Christ, I don't care what he says to you. But I have to know if I'm crazy."

I said, "George, there is no way to exaggerate the seriousness of what's happening to me. Do you understand that?"

Of course there was no way, either, to exaggerate the seriousness of what was happening to him. What did he think, about himself, about me, about the future? I don't know. I doubt that he knew.

Wednesday Nov. 19th

Because I want so much to go ahead, to get it all down, I haven't stopped long enough to say anything about how George and I lived during this period. It strikes me, though, thinking back, that although I spent every single private moment, every second I could spare from the outside world, from my work, my obligations, every hour that George was out of the house, thinking about the letters, resisting the compulsion to open them when they came, to search for them after George opened them and hid them, still, like leaves sailing across a pond on a windy day, our lives went on.

I am a full professor at my college now and I take my responsibilities seriously, no matter that education has come to seem outlandish to me. Some semesters I teach six hours, some nine. I take part in faculty meetings, serve on committees, keep office hours, make myself available to students, to some of whom I become deeply attached. I prepare my lectures, keep up with the critical literature, read new novels.

Once, somewhere along the line, I took a semester's sabbatical. I spent my time on the road, rushing from distraction to distraction. But day to day, week to week, I was working, just as George was.

In the evenings we went occasionally to the movies or to cocktail and dinner parties. We invited friends in for supper, as we always had, played an occasional game of poker, played double solitaire with each other, watched the television, even went fishing together. I could still read. For awhile George had great difficulty concentrating on books, but then, after the reconciliation, he went back to his poetry.

I took my turn with him shopping for groceries and cooking.

I gossiped with my friends about other people's marriages and affairs; about departmental crises; argued about politics, wrote protest letters to my congressman, worked on the telephone bank in state and national elections.

I swung my foot a lot. I tried to avoid occasions where I would have to sit and pretend to be listening to anything—music, lectures, readings, whatever. But except for a few things like that, I led my own perfectly ordinary life:

"How are you?"

"Fine. *Fine.* And you?"

"Corinne! I haven't seen you in ages. How are you?"

"Great!"

"And George?"

"Thriving."

"Still teaching, Corinne?"

"Of course. What would I do with myself if I weren't?"

"How are the children?"

"Great!"

"Everybody coming home for Christmas?"

You know how that kind of thing goes.

Thursday Nov. 20th

But at home, alone . . . .

The letters kept coming.

As soon as George was out of the house I would begin my methodical search for them.

I had warned him, hadn't I? I would not steal them when they came. I would not open them before he saw them. But if I found them . . .

I would find out the truth, the objective truth. I would base my life on the truth.

Don't ask me how I knew they were there—in my house. It was as if they—the letters—had seeds of plutonium in them and I were a living Geiger counter. My own ticking, the beating of my heart told me they were in my house.

He had not troubled to have them sent elsewhere. He would not trouble to destroy them. Perhaps he had not even heard me when I said I was losing my honor, my mind. Certainly he did not believe me.

If my heart could detect their presence, then it would beat even faster, louder, when I drew near to their hiding place. It was a matter of time, patience.

I began in the bookcases. I shook every book in the house and looked behind it. I went through the three-drawer file where George keeps mementos from college days, old theater programs, annuals, snapshot albums from high school. I looked in the chests of drawers in the children's deserted bedrooms. I went methodically through the contents of George's closet, looked in the pockets of his out-of-season clothes, went to the garage—the lower story of the old carriage house and garçon-nière—looked in the closet where he kept his gardening equipment and his tool boxes.

Again I have stopped writing, wandered through the house, looked out the windows. Cold weather now. We've installed a wood-burning heater in the old parlor fireplace and storm windows on the north side of the house, caulked and tightened everything to conserve energy. The winter sunshine streams in the south windows and glints softly off the worn floors that George sanded and stained and varnished again just five years ago. Everything is comfortable here and warm. A small fire burns on the hearth in our bedroom, where I like best to work. We've put in one of those new-fangled glass fire screens so as not to lose heat up the chimney.

I'm stumped. No longer about the location of the letters—about what it all meant.

Would I do it again? Have I learned anything? Does anyone ever learn anything?

Usually what I want to say comes tumbling out, once I make up my mind to say it, but this business—what can I say about it that's true?

The first, maybe the only thing that's true is that I don't understand . . .

No. I do understand—some things about myself—what I felt and wanted.

I wanted him to be mine alone. No matter that some part of me knew it was impossible, ridiculous. I had to know everything that went on with him. I wanted to possess his soul. Maybe I believed that his soul was captive inside the envelopes that contained those letters the boy wrote him. He received them, he read them, he folded his soul up with the sheets of paper and put it and them in the envelope and put the envelope in his inside jacket pocket over his heart and finally he hid them where I could never never find them.

And I had to know if I was crazy. I thought of other approaches to the second part of my problem. I would follow him on one of his trips to see the boy, would knock on the motel room door, force my way in . . . What motel? I didn't even know. You see how ridiculous? Or I would wait until the boy's next visit here, follow them, wait until they settled down someplace, and . . . And what?

I would hire a detective.

Jesus Christ!

You can see that reading the letters was the most practical, the least expensive way of finding out if I was crazy.

And what, what, what can I say about George that's true?

Did he marry me because some deep part of him rang like a neighboring bell to the vibrations of my obsessive heart? Did the bell sing to him softly that one day, one day I would pursue him, as he had pursued me, as I had pursued that other unattainable lover, the lover of my youth? Did it sing that he, too, could hide himself, evade me, escape me, teach me the limits of a woman's power?

Oh, George, my darling, my poor, muddled, suffering, obsessed, stony-hearted darling, you were in love. Maybe you're still in love. I don't know. I still don't know. Maybe you'll love him—him only—until you die.

Maybe, still, at night, holding me in your arms, gently moving your hand along my back, massaging every vertebra, pressing my legs against your groin, you think of him.

No. It must be then, most of all, that you block out every thought of him—of his hard young body, his bearded face, the roughness, urgency with which he seizes you, shakes from you the passion you have always denied me.

Friday Nov. 21st

George and I were fucking again.

Items for exploration in the Sexual Appendix:

A. How and why does the prospect of an encounter with a lover improve performance with a wife? We're talking here, you know, about synapses and electrical currents and chemical changes, about eager blood, a happy, shapely, compact prostate gland.

B. What part is played by the consciousness of power—the power to deceive and undeceive? By pity? Where are these located?

C. How and why does the knowledge of betrayal trigger the opening of legs, rolling over to be scratched?

D. Who is more powerful—betrayer or betrayed?

E. Who's in there pulling the strings?

F. Why did he—or I—decide that it matters even one jot where he puts that frail limp worm, that iron tool? Whether or how I receive it or another?

And what is the force that binds us to each other, enwraps us like a web of steel and nylon, a gill net for catching channel cat, a line, a hundred-pound test, strong enough to land a swordfish, a shark, a dolphin?

Later

So I believed that the reason why he had not destroyed the letters, the reason why he would never have kept them any place except in his own house was that they contained his soul.

But if he was keeping them, then where?

They kept coming, one every week.

134

Thinking it through, going methodically over each room, I told myself that I had exhausted every possibility.

But then I remembered. In the detached wing, above the garage, above what had once been the carriage house and the old kitchen—those storage rooms had never crossed my mind. Neither of us ever went up there except to put away what was too large to store in the main house, or to drag down some discarded piece of furniture for one of the children. That was the place.

One chilly afternoon—George gone for a twenty-four-hour shift—I put on an old pair of jeans and a sweater and jacket and climbed the enclosed stairway in the garage to take a look. Evidently, since I dressed for the occasion, I must have intended to make a thorough search.

It had been years since I had spent more than ten consecutive minutes in those rooms—since I'd even looked at them—not since the children years ago used them for a clubhouse or a pretend ship or desert island to which they occasionally invited me for a visit.

The roof here—the wing is a story and a half with dormers looking out over the levee behind our house—slants down in strange ways and the studs jut up to make little alcoves and irregularly shaped rooms. One dormer seems to be sitting among the branches of the sycamore tree that grows just outside the garage doors. The white bones of its bare branches make a pattern against the pale blue winter sky.

Dust and cobwebs everywhere, and stacks of old boxes and trunks—some of them are ours, some, full of newspapers and magazines dating back to the late eighteen hundreds and early nineteen hundreds, were here when we moved in. Near the stair is a crib we bring down whenever a grandchild comes for a visit.

The walls have probably not been painted since the last "garçon" called it a garçonnière sometime in the late nineteenth century. My own children, at some point or other when their secret society met here, painted warnings on the walls:

Death to Intruders in red paint, *Tuesday Is the Day*, and a couple of others equally cryptic.

I crossed the room to the dormer by the sycamore tree, sat down on the dusty wooden window seat, and looked out. It was like being in a tree house, high, enclosed, and wild. A lookout. I was up here, like a child, among bare branches, could look down on whoever came and went below, could see the path that ran along by the river on the other side of the levee where the teenagers straggled home from school in the afternoons. As I sat gazing out the window, a young girl came along the top of the levee, carrying books, paused and looked, as it seemed, at me, hidden away where she could not see me. Then she put down her books by the path and ran down the levee to the water's edge. I could see only her back now, slender waist, legs concealed under jeans; long, straight brown hair hanging almost to her waist. She seemed to be looking out over the water, dreaming there. Beyond her a towboat pushed a string of barges northward through the still water. In a few minutes I saw a boy quartering the slope of the levee downward to where she stood. He took her hand. *To be so young again.* I turned away.

With very little expense I could make this place into a delightful apartment. Yes, I might move in up here. I would have to go through the boxes, methodically, decide what to keep, what to throw away. I would find the letters and . . .

I really was crazy. The project for a few minutes seemed possible. I would make this place my own. Then what? God knows.

I went downstairs, got my green stone and brought it up. I opened the lid of the dormer window seat, which concealed a storage box full of bound journals, papers and magazines, and put my stone inside, at the very bottom of the box, under the magazines.

My guilt and nuttiness were such that I was sure if I left even a footprint in the dust on the floor here, George would notice it when he came the following week to hide his letter. Then he would take all the letters away, would deny me the truth again. When I thought of this, I grabbed an old paintbrush and began to walk out backwards like an Indian concealing a trail, blending my footprints with the dust.

What about his footprints? Did you look for them?

Of course there were faint prints. But he'd been up to bring the crib down and then to return it, and . . .

How could you have it both ways? Move into the garage and at the same time keep G. from knowing you were looking for the letters there?

I was crazy, I tell you, crazy. I couldn't, of course, have it both ways. I gave up the notion of moving in. But I couldn't give up the search. A couple of days later I went back up there and started to work. I began to sneeze. I got filthy dirty. It was all ridiculous, ridiculous. I couldn't be crazy after all, or not here. As soon as I took the first stack of *National Geographics* from their box and began to hold them by the covers and shake them (to shake out the letters), as soon as I saw the holes, children, where you had cut out pictures of the Yangtze River Delta, relief maps of the Ural Mountains, I knew it was ridiculous. George would no more have trotted up into this cobweb-shrouded gloom to hide anything than I would have.

And in the course of that brief exploration, I was distracted from my madness. I saw that the old papers and magazines were crumbling to ruin. Something should be done about them. There was a rat's nest in one trunk. In the window box where I'd put my stone I saw a couple of ledgers of George's great-grandfather's that clearly should be preserved.

The next day I went down to the local historical society headquarters, got a couple of rat- and mildew-proof boxes, stopped by the health department and got some rat poison, and came home.

When I emptied the window box to get out the ledgers and throw away the rat-gnawed magazines among which they were lying, one of the boards in the bottom of the box tipped downward. My stone slipped along the tipping board toward and through the opening between the studs. Half fearfully (spiders? rats? at the very least, roaches?) I tipped the board higher, pulled it out, and reached down into the space between the bottom of the window seat storage box and the subflooring. It was there that I found the diary.

Not George's diary, of course. As you must know by now, the keeping of a diary would be foreign to George's nature. It was his grandmother's diary, the diary of the courageous horsewoman, the gallant widow, the loving mother, the suicide.

Saturday Nov. 22nd

The diary that follows was in two old-fashioned, cardboard-bound school notebooks. It had not been kept with any regularity, only, it appeared, when she had been in town visiting. This house, of course, was her parents' home.

There was a lapse between the entries in the first notebook and the single long entry in the second, the first dating from the last year of her marriage and ending with her husband's death, the second ten years later.

Here it is then:

April 3. I cannot trust myself. How could I have married him? Surely even at sixteen I should have had sufficient judgment . . .

April 4. When at last I come here, to this house—not my home, I have no home—when I am away from him for a short while, I feel myself compelled to climb up here, to conceal myself from everyone. I wish never, never to come out again. Ah, I remember when this was Brother George's room, when I used to visit him here, how we would sit in front of the fire and crack pecans and he would talk foolishness, nothing but foolishness, and so would I.

April 5. Could Mama not have seen what he would be like? Father?

April 6. A woman's life in this time and place . . . How can I say how I loathe my life? To be what I am, trapped here in this body. No god could have meant his creature, made in his likeness, to endure such a life. I think daily of death, of peace, of the infinite deep joy of sleep. But my babies? What would happen to my babies?

139

April 7. It is true. I am with child again.

April 11. Why am I here in this empty room, at this dusty table, writing? I cannot show my words to anyone, cannot talk to anyone. All I can do is write in these pages, these words and hide them away . . . Mama, oh, if you found them, what could you do except suffer for me? Or condemn me. Is that what I want?

April 12. Yesterday I sent to Louise and she came secretly and gave me a dose of a decoction she had made from the roots of the cotton plant. Afterwards I had Jimmie saddle Eagle and went for a very long ride—trotted, cantered, galloped. No result.

April 13. I threw myself down the front steps yesterday, again without result. I told Mama I had stumbled over a toy. I bruised my shoulder and my wrist feels as if it may be cracked. Henry came and put a light splint on it.

April 17. Three days ago I miscarried twins in the privy. I will not speak of this to Clarence—or anyone. As it is clear that I am unwell, Mama is sending Jimmie to the country with a message for Clarence that I will stay in town a week or two longer. I spend my days reading to myself and to the children, receiving callers. I told Mama my period is unusually heavy and I must stay quiet. She knows well enough what happened.

April 20. Clarence requests that we return to the country.

April 21. Why do I write here? I must intend that someone, some time, read my words.

I am twenty-four years old. I have borne seven children and buried three. I have induced in myself two miscarriages. *I am twenty-four years old and I have buried three children.* One born dead, unnamed, a perfect child, strangled by the cord—as if I had complicity in it. Little Caroline, my bird, my wren, dead before her first birthday. Oliver, so healthy at first, weaned, cherished through his second summer, dead of scarlet fever before he was three. Let me remember these graves.

Clarence says this burden is the lot of women. He means the burden of becoming pregnant; he does not seem to understand that one feels severely the loss of small children. He himself avoids them, to avoid the pain of loss, and advises me to harden my heart against the unborn, to detach myself from the infant. No doubt he speaks truly. I will bear more, miscarry more, bury more, before the blessed hour when blood no longer flows from my womb.

April 28. He requires us to return. He will be in to fetch us on Monday next.

May 3. He spent the evening after supper explaining to Mama and Father and me the limitations of the female soul. Mama knitted. Father nodded. He gave me a book to read: *The Proper Conduct of Christian Wives.* My hatred is poisoning me. I will die of it.

May 4. My impulses are insane. I know I must acknowledge to myself the circumstances of my life and accept them. I have four living children. I must not allow myself to forget even for a moment my responsibilities to them.

July 8. We are back in town, but he is with us. The danger of malaria and even, God forbid, yellow fever, drove us out of the country. The winter was unusually dry and there is no more winter water in the cisterns. The servants are catching summer water, but I will not allow the children to drink that fever-infested water. He will not stay long, I hope, but will have to go to attend to his farming.

The ride into town was not so bad as I had feared it might be. In most cases I can manipulate his mood through flattery and prevent his becoming abusive with either me or the children. He is stupid.

But sometimes—oh, how treacherous my nature is—it comes into my head to provoke him deliberately, to contradict him, defy him, make fun of him, show him how I despise him. I was able to resist today. Such behavior is without value either to me or to the children.

July 9. He explained to me again last night that woman

is like the fig tree and wrote out for me again the Biblical reference, recommending it as my Bible reading this morning. It is man's duty to fructify the blossom nightly, daily—sometimes, it seems to me, hourly.

July 10. I hate, hate, hate him. If I could not write down my hatred, I would swell like a toad with the poison and die of it. I hate his piety, his learning, his "goodness," all of which he does not fail to congratulate himself on. I hate his condescension, the bullying way he has with servants and children. I hate his pointed nose, his breath, smelling of tobacco and rotten teeth, his strength.

July 11. Last night he entered me in my sleep from behind, jerked me onto my knees and was inside me almost before I woke. I was sleeping deeply, very weary as we had ridden out to Poplar Hill to call on his aunt, taking the children with us; and I had had to be constantly alert to quiet them on the way home. He was sleeping, and is, of course, particularly sarcastic and even brutal toward them if they waken him.

He prefers this position, he says, as one enters more deeply and therefore is more likely to impregnate. Also, although he does not mention this, my situation is that of a bitch under a dog. I know he wants to feel his power over me. Although I would prefer not to be violated in my sleep, this position pleases me, too. I do not have to see his face, smell his breath, feel anything of him but disembodied hands, a bodiless cold iron tool forcing its way in, pounding at my womb, and then it is over.

July 12. When I married, no one had told me how children are made or how they come into the world. My education was entrusted to him. I will not consign a daughter of mine to such a fate. Not even George, who loves me, I am sure, prepared me for the wedding night. How could he—a man, my brother? Mama said vaguely that all women must submit themselves to their husbands. Father read the Bible. It would have been better for me if I had had an older sister.

But women, I believe, must will themselves to continue in such ignorance, in order to fulfill the expectations of the world. Surely, having seen dogs mount, bulls with cows, roosters, I should have drawn some inference. I remember Mama or Irene saying of animals, "Oh, they're just fighting, honey." Yes, I was willfully ignorant. I invited my fate.

July 22. My God! He is dead. He is dead. Everything is mine, all mine—my life, my children's lives, the farm. I own myself. I am in charge of my life, of my children.

July 23. No pieties. I am forced to tolerate enough of those downstairs. I am in charge of my life. I own myself. And the children—oh, I will cherish them. And oh, no more will come, only to die. I am looking out of the window into the woods by the levee. The leaves on the poplar trees leap in the wind like green flames. The hawks are sailing high in the blue day. The wind blows. He is dead and I am alive.

July 24. I will be lonely, Oh, the blessed, lovely loneliness, the sacred solitude. Oh, I will sleep alone. I am on my knees. I am saying prayers of thanksgiving. He is dead.

This was the last entry in the first notebook. The second notebook is in the same hand, undated, and contains only one long entry:

It has been some years now since I have come to Brother George's room to write. How many? Eight? Ten? Ruth is sixteen. Clarence died when she was six.

To begin with, there was no time. Work kept me far from town and from the leisure for reflection that these visits provided. But that, of course, was the least of it. I had nothing to say, no need. I was happy in my work, my life. All went well those first years. It was as if the children and I had at last found a sane world where it was possible to live and be content. I wanted nothing more than to work myself to exhaustion, cherish my children, sleep alone.

Now, all has gone by the board, and I am here again. I

have reread and laid aside that earlier diary, thought again about those years, how I came here, to this refuge, to speak to myself. Yes, I understand, as I did not then, that those pages were a cry—a desperate cry—from myself to myself, hidden here where only I in my solitude could hear my own voice. And I know well, too, why I write now. I know why I will leave this notebook hidden here. I have no one to give it to, no one to whom I may allow myself to speak out. Not my daughters. I cannot bear to speak to my daughters. God keep them from the need to understand my life. But I will leave these pages, will put down the record, as Crusoe, alone on his island, put down his record, not knowing who might find it after his solitary life was spent.

I do not speak to myself now, but to you, whoever you are—in your need if you are a woman, in your arrogance if you are a man.

I stop here, sisters, to think who it may be who will find my record. If you are a man, you must be one who is tearing down this house. There would be no other reason why a man would pull the boards from the bottom of this box. Take the notebooks home, my friend, give them to your wife, your sister, your mother, as a curiosity. You are too busy to labor over the fading script. But unless the house is torn down, I think you, finder, are a woman. You have taken the papers, the journals, out of the box to scrub it. You bear down with your scrubbing brush. The board tips. Here I am.

Sisters, reading, I charge you, do not turn away from this reflection of your loneliness, your despair.

I know that many women live as I did with Clarence and as I do now, year after year in isolation from all other human beings, all equals, all peers. Children, warm children, children's arms and bodies, but all else—solitude. No man, no woman, to stand facing you, eye to eye, hold out a hand and say, Speak to me, sister, fellow traveler, sufferer, fellow human creature. Reveal yourself to me. I lived in just such solitude during the eight years of my marriage. Now, after one brief interlude, I live thus again.

Four years after Clarence died, my cousin Maria came from Atlanta and brought her son with her for an extended visit. She had come two years earlier for a briefer stay and at that time, although we had not seen each other since we were in convent school together in our early teens, we had found we were congenial companions. We had been fond of each other as children, had had one of those passionate girlhood friendships, and had corresponded over the years. This second visit she planned to stay some weeks, perhaps even months, as her husband, who is a cotton factor, had gone to Liverpool on an extended business trip.

Now, as she told me shortly after she arrived, her circumstances had changed. Indeed, her predicament with regard to her marriage, although it was very different from what mine had been, was in its way equally distressing.

My invisible, my unknown sister, for whom I write, I ask you this question: Did God indeed mean women to be subject to men? I do not for one moment believe it. Oh, how isolated we are, each in her cage. Out there, in the world, there must be places where a woman's life is different. I know there must be. How strange it is that we all consent together to abandon control of ourselves, that men consent with us in this corrupting exercise of power.

Here is a story that my grandmother told me. When she was a young married woman, one of her friends married a man who had a large plantation in the remote northern part of the county. As the years passed, my grandmother's friend came less and less often to town. It was a half-day's ride in the buggy, her parents died, and she had no close relatives. The husband, who had always been thought eccentric, was not one to exchange visits around the county as other people did, staying for days and even weeks. He kept his wife at home. My grandmother wrote letters to her friend and sent them out by families who lived in that neighborhood and who came occasionally to town, but she never received an answer. She concluded that her friend's attention was on other matters and wrote no more. More years passed and word came that the young woman, who by now had two small daughters, had suddenly been taken ill and had died before the husband could fetch her to town to the doctor. This, of course, in those early days, was not unusual. The little girls were eight and nine when their mother died or, as I now believe, was murdered. The neighbors, none nearer than five or six miles away, reported that the father grew increasingly surly. The occasional visitor was not invited into the house. Now and then someone reported seeing the little girls playing outside under the eye of a Negro woman who must have been their mammy.

One night, some five years after the woman's death, fox hunters . . .

Do the men in your time, sister, still hunt foxes in the night, sitting around the fire in the woods while the horses stamp and snort, listening to the dogs bell, drinking whisky, telling stories, while the fox runs, runs, pants, scrambles, stumbles, leads the dogs far from her den, where the young will starve when she fails to come home in the morning?

But let me continue the story. I have no wish to sound hysterical or to be accused of sensationalism.

Two fox hunters, riding in the woods, were startled one night when two young girls burst out of a thicket by the path and stopped like wraiths, ghosts, almost under their horses' hooves. The sisters were being used by their father as foxes in a sport similar to that the hunters were engaged in. The dogs were the black men on the place. The prize was not the brush.

Horrified at the young girls' garbled tale, the hunters took them up on their saddles, took them home to their wives, who fed and washed and cared for them. The next day, taking the children with them (I say children; they were fourteen and fifteen), probably out of the fear that their father might come and claim them if they were left behind with the women, the men went into town. The girls were left in my grandmother's care while the men gathered with their peers and consulted what steps to take next. Later that day a deputation called on the father and advised him that he had twenty-four hours to get out of the county and that if ever he were seen in the area again, he would be shot. The girls, the men decided, should be sent off to a convent school in St. Louis, far from the scandalous scenes of their childhood, where no.one would know their tainted history. They went. There they did, in fact, respond to kindness and attention and a wholesome diet. They received the rudiments of an education. They were taught how to dress and how to conduct themselves in civilized society. Both of them, in spite of their lack of money and connections, made fairly good marriages. They were lovely little things, my grandmother said, had no trouble finding beaus.

I know nothing of their later lives or how they got along with their husbands, but I know this. My grandmother told the story in the belief that the ending was a happy one. She had no need to inquire into their later circumstances. They married. Nor did she wonder whether their father—the monster—went elsewhere and established a new ménage with a new wife to abuse and new daughters to destroy.

I once asked what happened to his property, but my grandmother was vague. "I suppose he must have had a lawyer," she said. "Someone must have sold it for him."

Evidently he would not have lacked money for a fresh start.

Can this story be true? Or is it a fairy tale that my grandmother heard from her mother, transformed, and came to believe? There is no way to know.

In any case, the story that I have to tell of Maria and me is true. Maria's husband, after she returned from her first visit to me, had informed her that while desiring to maintain a respectable family establishment for his child's sake, he would no longer have carnal relations with her. She was left to draw her own conclusions with regard to his reasons. Very likely he maintained some other establishment in which his carnal needs were satisfied. But she was a passionate woman and she longed for the warmth of a man's body in her bed, for love, for children.

We were alone together, she and I, sisters in loneliness and pain, and we came to love each other. We determined between ourselves to make our stand, and we did. I had control of my property, as she did not of hers, and I "hired" her as my "companion." She and the child, a beautiful little boy whom I came easily to love, stayed on with us when the husband returned from Liverpool. She wrote to him that she required nothing from him, that, indeed, if he liked, she would be willing to return to Atlanta periodically to grace his table, act as his hostess, maintain the façade that was important to him; and from time to time she did.

But he wanted the boy under his control and she would not give in or give up the child.

The depth of his capacity for vindictiveness was something that neither she nor I had anticipated, although I, with my knowledge of my own husband, should surely have had little reason for optimism regarding the impulses in the soul of a man.

He was prepared to destroy us both.

It was easy for him to do. He suborned not one, but two of my servants, who gave testimony in a private custody hearing regarding Maria's and my connection and our sleeping arrangements. He even enlisted my own father in his conscienceless scheme, filling him with nonsense about the corruption of my children, especially of William, who is just into his teens. With the reality of an unfavorable custody decision hanging over her, Maria, in order to keep her son, returned to her husband's house.

The evidence is in the court records. My father is determined that he will take my children from me. He has gone, in fact, this very week, to Atlanta, to discuss me with Maria's husband and enlist his testimony in a new hearing, before the same judge, with regard to my unfitness as a parent. I, on my part, came into town yesterday, when I learned that he had gone, to lay all this before my mother, hoping that I might persuade her to use her leverage against him. I believe, if she threatened to leave him, to come to me, he would desist. He wants, not inconvenience, or a scandal, but control.

But she looks at me and weeps. She looks at me and weeps.

The terms which my father has offered me are that I leave my children to his guardianship and depart this area and that he, in turn, will commit himself to manage my property and send me a stipend for my support. The children, he says, will not be told of my "sin." But it is unthinkable that they should continue under my pernicious influence. Perhaps, he says, we can agree on some story to tell them. He is still mulling this over. I have now fixed upon a story he can use.

Have I had anything to say thus far in regard to my father's character? No. And indeed, I find it difficult to write about him. My father is no monster. He is a man. Or, more accurately, he does not intend to behave in a monstrous way, but to do his duty. I understand his fears for his grandchildren, his revulsion from his unnatural daughter. I do understand. And then, too, perhaps he has felt some nagging fear of and revulsion from me for years—ever since I proved capable of living without a man, of managing my own affairs. And no one anywhere has ever suggested to him that he might try to be different.

Still, I think about his religion, the Bible that he pores over every evening—the religion, the Bible of the gentle Jesus. He swears every oath by the religion of love and forgiveness.

"Let him who is without sin . . ."

So that even from his point of view this treatment of me is monstrous. While from mine . . .

Ah, sisters, is contentment a sin? Is tenderness a sin? Gentleness? Cherishing? Joy? Ecstasy?

But this hatred in my heart now is a sin. And I cannot

purge myself of it. Still in my heart, after years, hard and pulsing as the iron tool he rent me with, as a lump of glowing iron, is the hatred I felt for him—for Clarence. I thought I had abandoned it. But I cherish it again. I feed it with memories of the violence he did us all, the contempt in which he held us. And now I set my father and Maria's husband in their places beside him in my heart. I hate them all. I cannot not hate them. My hatred is burning through my heart into my flesh, burning a hole in my side, the lump of burning iron is living in my side.

Clarence took from me my self, made me into nothing.

And now he—they—will take my children.

Who could invent a tale dreadful enough to be equal to the real perfidy, the heartlessness, the hypocrisy, the self-righteousness of real men?

Sisters in pain, whatever your circumstances, whatever the time, I charge you, hate them. Torment them.

And now I have determined . . .

Again, no. Just as there was no Toad, there was no diary. Or rather, the diary is mine, my invention.

I did go up to those old storage rooms and look for George's letters and I did not find them. That much is true. I sat on the window seat one winter afternoon in the chill early dusk and watched the children straggle home from school along the path by the stagnant waters of our river and I thought about her. Wondered again about her.

But I invented it all. A plausible—what seemed to me plausible—explanation of the mystery of her death. It was based, I said to myself, on my knowledge of her times, my knowledge of our families. I sat at my table near the fire in my sunny bedroom and wrote her diary.

Here are some verifiable facts on which I based my invention.

My own great-grandmother bore fifteen children between the time she married at seventeen and her forty-third birthday. She buried eight before maturity, buried them at all ages from birth to puberty, one, her beloved youngest daughter, in childbirth at seventeen. The stones stand in the cemetery. My twins are buried in the same lot. Their stone stands there also. My great-grandmother died senile in her middle eighties, toward the end thought she was a child, kept looking for her mother.

An old great-aunt told me the Gothic tale of the two girls and the sadistic father in the woods. She said it was true and she gave us all the names, even the married names of the two daughters. She told it to you, too, George; and I have told it to you, children. I know you have all heard it. She may have read it somewhere or made it up or it may indeed be true. She was the one who died believing she was a prisoner in a whore-house. Remember? But she told us this tale before she was crazy.

I have glanced through *The Proper Conduct of Christian Wives* (epigraph from 1st Corinthians: "And if they will learn anything, let them ask their husbands"). Books like this sold thousands of copies in the middle and late eighteen hundreds and were in a large number of family bookcases, particularly among certain pious provincial families with vague pretensions and little education.

All the rest, all, I invented. It poured out of me like water from a spout. I did not think.

Again, you must see, it's a way of putting off. But something else as well. Is the dream third of my life taking over? My dreams of my own frustration, impotence, passivity, hatred, imprisonment, death?

Saturday Nov. 29th

Yes, her story came easily—like automatic writing—just as The Toad's story did. But oh, believe me, not just at the beginning, but with every word I meant to tell the truth—*a* truth. I began, I wrote on, and in some secret part of me, some hollow hidden even from my own probing, I must have known the writing would lead us here.

I sit staring at the paper.

Twenty-two years ago—you were five, Corinne . . .

Later

If I am incapable of putting everything down, as it seems to me to have happened, if I persist in deceiving you about the very center of our lives, what can I say, what can I know?

I think again of my childhood, of my confession that summer day to having gone to *The Unholy Three*, of the agony of guilt before confession, of the moment in my mother's presence, the four o'clock sunshine slanting through the south window, the drowsy tick of the lawn mower blades, the smell of cut grass. Through the window I see the slowly moving figure of the old man who cut the grass. Back and forth he moves, passing and repassing the window with dreamlike slowness, as slow as if he were walking under water.

My mother lays her warm hand on my shoulder, says, "Well, apparently it didn't hurt you, my dear. You're not having nightmares, are you?"

But my brother and my mother said it never happened. They said it never happened.

What can we do, friends, darlings, if there are no memories?

153

How will you know me, children? How will you know yourselves?

Will we all finish the day, as I so often do, sitting, each one alone, at the kitchen table, in the deepest hour of darkness, gazing at the ghosts in the box? Will the box come to flicker in our heads instead of our own memories?

Later

Here's another thing. Maybe we make up our lives like stories. George's grandmother was there, sleeping in the parish roll book, waiting for me to make up my life and assign her her place in it, to round out her story and bring it to its true close. And George? Does he make up his life to match mine, mine to match his?

Later

I have the green stone on my desk, James, the one you gave me in the dream, the one I found in reality by the laurel tree; and it has turned out to be a stone to crack George's skull with, to crush his genitals, to pound him to death.

Tuesday Dec. 2nd

Yesterday in the bank, where I'd gone to deposit my salary check, I met a young man who was a high school friend of William's. He had on sunglasses and to begin with I was not sure who he was, although I saw something familiar about the set of his mouth, the way he held his head. Then he spoke, called my name, asked about the boys and Corinne.

The sunglasses were the mirrored kind behind which the eyes of the wearer are invisible. As we talked, I had to knot my hands together behind me to keep from reaching out, snatching them off. I saw only myself, doubly reflected in the lenses, nodding, smiling insanely with wide clown mouths. The tops of my heads expanded and contracted every time either of us moved, like expanding and deflating balloons, my forehead bled off into a void, my cheeks below staring eyes were as knobby and wide apart as a Russian peasant's, my chins as long as Andrew Jackson's. Behind me in the lenses whorls of beige and caramel-streaked marble wavered under expanding and contracting banks of lights.

I could think of nothing except that I had to get away, anywhere, before I screamed at him to take them off. I'm not in there! It's you, you! You!

Why not throw this all away—put every page in the fire, close the empty notebook, put it in my desk? What use can any of it be to anyone?

Thursday Dec. 11th

We are rich people, George and I. I have never in my life gone hungry or been severely uncomfortable for more than a few days at a time. Childhood pneumonia, a hemorrhoidectomy, childbirth—but real hopeless physical anguish, helplessness before suffering? Only when I kept watch at my mother's long death, and dreadful as that was, my mother was old, had lived out her life. Oh, thank God, I have never had the anguish of watching helpless as my own child suffered, saw death bear down.

I am not different in these respects from hundreds of thousands, even millions, of people in my class, my country, my time.

George is not in precisely the same case. He was trapped, a medic, ten days in an isolated field hospital in the Battle of the Bulge, not knowing hour to hour whether he would be alive the next. He worked eighteen hours a day caring for the wounded, sleeping in his clothes, living on benzedrine. Morphine ran out, blood plasma ran out. He watched men die in agony whom elsewhere he, a second-year medical student, could have saved. And now, of course, now, too, he lives a professional life of alternate crisis and boredom, suffering and euphoria. He works to exhaustion or waits out his shift reading whodunits—says he can't read poetry in the hospital. He lays his professional life on the line, continues to take risks when he has to.

But, even so, he comes home to security.

Here we are, sitting in our comfortable living room, playing gin rummy, a fire burning low on our hearth, our children out in the world pursuing the lives they choose to pursue, our own niches in our professions shaped to suit our needs, our preferences.

Surely we should smile at each other, look stoically on the looming inevitability of death, clasp hands gently, enjoy each other in our declining years. We are fortunate.

In Somalia, in Cambodia, in Chad, millions of people die of starvation every year. Political prisoners languish, suffer torture, are murdered, in Chile and Argentina, in South Africa and San Salvador. There is nothing he or I can do about these dreadful human scandals—is there?—except give money to Amnesty International, support UNESCO.

And, closer home: In the salt domes in South Louisiana they may soon be storing nuclear wastes, which will seep into the water table of the surrounding parishes. At Port Gibson, Mississippi, they are building a nuclear power plant meant to house the largest reactor in the world. A few years ago a tornado struck the cooling tower and ripped it apart like a Lego toy. This unfortunate accident has not deterred the builders from pursuing their Faustian dreams.

In the fall, when I am driving home from a symposium on Thoreau—"The world is well kept; no rubbish accumulates; the morning air is clear, and no dust has settled on the grass. Behold how the evening now steals over the fields, the shadows of the trees creeping farther and farther into the meadows, and erelong the stars will come to bathe in these retired waters. Her undertakings are secure and never fail . . ."—the stench of rotting vegetation, the poisonous stink of defoliants make the land reek like a gigantic silage trench.

These are matters about which public decisions must be made. We can vote, of course, can protest, but our lives are lived at another level, are they not?

Last week from George's hospital a bill for $87,000 went out to the estate of old Mr. Pickett, one of our retired bankers. They had done everything in their power to save the old man —he was ninety-one—but after three months in the hospital, eighty-one days in intensive care, his lion heart, as the church bulletin put it, gave out.

That same day on Redbud Street a twenty-eight-year-old woman left her nine children locked in the house while she went dancing with her boyfriend. The house caught fire. All the children died. Firemen said they heard pounding, a few muffled cries inside, but the fire went so fast, the children couldn't have suffered long.

One of my students resigned from the college last week. He is suffering his third paranoid schizophrenic breakdown and believes that the government has hired him to reenact the murder of Martin Luther King. Through this reenactment, his controlling case officer assures him, the real truth about the conspiracy will come out and the FBI will be exonerated.

What am I saying? That our personal lives are without value or significance because real human suffering is so staggering? Surely not that. For ultimately all people suffer and die only as themselves.

That we should give all we have to the poor and follow Him? Oh, if only we could, if only I could be shut forever of my horrid petty obsessions, my loathsome self.

That, like the magical kings and queens of old, we must love one another, lust after one another, cherish one another, indulge one another, lie down in the fields and fornicate so that the land will be fertile and the poisons washed away?

That we must put hands and feet and lips and foreheads together and live as brother and sister, man and wife, in child-like trust? Let down the milk in our breasts, raise up the child in our arms?

Yes, I think we must all do that, somehow.

But how?

Can you help us, children? How are you managing? Have you any advice?

Thursday Jan. 1st

I will begin again. Twenty-two years ago—you were five, Corinne—I fell in love with a woman who was married to a professor at the college. You knew them: Judith and Lee. Now. I have written a sentence, two sentences. I have taken the first step.

I am not . . .

The love of women is not my natural bent.

That word—natural—is wrong. All I can say is that I loved her.

I prefer sex with a man to sex with a woman. I feel no particular pleasure when I touch a woman's breasts, although I suppose I would feel pleasure if a cat licked mine. Unlike the woman in my diary, I delight in the weight of a man's hard body, his breath on my face, the piercing moment of entry, the "iron tool." These days, when George comes to me, I'm ready—awake, asleep, frontwards, backwards or upside down.

What happened, then? How did it come about that I got involved, in the middle of my marriage, in a long love affair with a woman?

Friday Jan. 2nd

Again and again, children, I've lined you up, thinking I can have an imaginary conversation with you. Someone will ask questions and we'll get to the bottom of it all. I see you, of course, with infinitely compassionate, understanding faces— but then I remember that in real life you ask perhaps understanding, but often embarrassing, searching questions: *First a Toad and then an imaginary grandmother and now a woman— a female lover? You're kidding, aren't you? And you expect us to keep on believing you—or even listening?*

How can I distill away from what I write the taint of coincidence, keep you from thinking, My God, she's as nutty as she claims to be? And what can I say in my own defense, how excuse myself for perverting my own deepest intent? For playing games with your love? May I plead my extremity, my . . .

But listen to me, if I'd reversed the order of telling, if I'd started with my past, would you have been any more likely to believe me? Of course not.

And that's not the only reason why I put off this final grotesque confession, why I didn't say at the beginning how things were—or seemed. I must have been afraid to put my attention on that faraway time. I thought I could leave it where it was—buried. But then, in spite of myself, I couldn't help pouring all the old devastating pain, all the ancient love and hate, into George's poor helpless dead grandmother.

And there's this I think of now, children. It's not fair to put these questions and answers in your mouths. Clearly, when I do, I'm only assuaging my own anxiety about what you'll think, whether you will turn away from me forever. But all the same,

I do see you and hear you—oh, I feel your dear presence in my life, as if you were in this room where I sit and write. So let me imagine one last time how you might speak, and then, afterwards, I'll speak only for myself.

We are together then, the four of us, late in the evening, as we so often are, when you are all at home at the same time. George is at work.

You, James, pick up the green stone from my desk and weigh it in your hand, looking down at it and then at me, your brown eyes full of pain and love. You are standing by the fireplace, the light from my desk lamp shining on your face and chestnut hair, glinting off a brassy streak and flecks of gold along one side of the stone. I had not noticed the streak of gold before (a layer of iron pyrites, maybe?), only the white veins, the patches of rust like lichen.

Corinne, you're folding your arms as your father does, drawing in a long leg, a high-arched foot, gazing at me out of alert, puzzled brown eyes. You hair, like mine when I was younger, is caught severely back, but the dark curls escape around your face. A pile of clean clothes, waiting to be folded, is tumbled in the basket by your chair. Across the room, sprawled on the daybed, the third Corinne—fourth, counting my grandmother; fifth, counting hers—has fallen from one instant to the next into sleep, face flushed, small legs bent at the knee, one arm trailing. Ah, how a sleeping child moves me, the image printed on my nerve cells like the memory of music.

William, you're listening almost as detachedly as you listened to Janice, as you listen to yourself. You're slender and fit as always, but bearded now, because I like your black pirate's beard and I can imagine you however I wish. You have just come from the kitchen, where you got a mango out of the icebox and you're holding it in your hand, turning it and laying it against your cheek, as if to test it for life. You give me a wry smile.

"Mama, how can this be?" you say. "How is it possible that anybody old enough to call a refrigerator an icebox has got herself into such a mess?"

Now, Corinne, I see you give the basket a kick. Diapers scatter across the floor. "Here's a different kind of question," you say. "Why is it that when you imagine me listening to your tale of woe, I'm suckling a child or folding clothes. William is singing. James is looking judicious. I'm folding clothes. Most of the time in my life I'm not folding clothes. I work, remember? I have an M.S. in math. I'm divorced. I have a lover of whom I'm fond, of whom you disapprove."

And I say in reply, "I don't disapprove of Stewart, Corinne."

"Never mind," you say. "I didn't mean I wanted to talk about myself—or him. But listen, you present yourself—I don't know—as passive. And me, too. You present me as if I were an extension of you."

"You have a temper, you know, Mama," William says. "Do you remember the day—how old was I? nine or ten?—when you stopped the car on the freeway and made us all get out and walk home because we wouldn't stop fighting in the back seat?"

"That wasn't on the freeway," I say. "It was on Spruce Street, not five blocks from home."

"You're strong," James says. "You're a powerful woman for a child to . . ."

"Not to change the subject," William says, "but it always seemed to me that you *presented* Daddy to us, as if he weren't capable of being himself, or as if we might not love him, if we knew what he was really like. That was a hell of a lot more important to me in my childhood than what you and Daddy did with your spare time."

"William, I . . ."

"Here's another thing," James says. "Corinne is irritated because you've got her folding diapers, but what about me? For your convenience, you've simply banished my wife, haven't you? It's too much trouble to say whether she's here or elsewhere. You haven't even given her a name."

"I don't object to standing on one leg for you like a parrot and eating a mango," William says, "but there it is, our lives have very little to do with any of this. We have our own problems, our own memories to struggle with."

"Is it really us you're thinking about—communicating with us?" Corinne says. "Aren't you bent—no matter how carefully you've tried to convince us that you're not—on destroying our love for our father? If that's your aim, then obviously you had a good reason for holding back the story of your affair, a reason you neglected to mention when you were listing reasons."

"Do you remember when you said you thought Daddy was the impossible, a truly monogamous man?" William says. "What huge pieces of his character did you edit out to be able to say so naïve a thing as that?"

"He edited his character, I didn't."

"Maybe you were just smug: *I'm more than enough for him.*"

"Or snide: *Poor fellow, he's undersexed.*"

Ah, children, I know you would never, never say these cruel things to me. Never. The questions, the comments, after all are mine, not yours.

Saturday Jan. 3rd

In another twenty years, if I'm still alive, will this present seem, as my long-ago life with Judith now seems, the life of a stranger to the data of which, mysteriously, I have access?

Here is how it began. I came to hate George. No matter that I trusted him, was fond of him, cherished him. I hated his nose that I love so passionately, hated the body that now, in the green summer mornings, the frigid winter dawns, I love to lean against, entwine with my own.

He would not let me in.

Who's in there, after all? Is there a monster, a hunchbacked dwarf over whom in very shame he draws the veil, whom he has never trusted me to love? Does he know who's in there? Has he always known?

There's the razor that slits the carotid artery, lets my blood pour out.

But, whatever he was or wanted, he vanished from our marriage.

True, he wanted me to be available. He wanted to come home to his sunny, green-lighted, tree-shaded house, to eat my good cooking (well, he's a good cook, too), to find that the wood was ordered for the winter, the car serviced, the homestead exemption signed; to sit down to a game of gin rummy, to read aloud to the children, to go to the sand bar and look for driftwood. But he would not let me in. He barricaded himself in his life and I hated him for it.

I see him now, the familiar grooves of weariness on either side of his nose, reaching down to his chin. I see his green eyes, dull with exhaustion, lighting up at the prospect of a peaceful hour digging in his garden, at a child's joke or the casual visit of some acquaintance he scarcely ever thought of, but not for me, never for me.

When he turned to me in the darkness, his need, his lust, seemed mechanical, anonymous, and I responded to it with a kind of raging frustration that I carefully and successfully concealed. Oh, how much more furious I was just because my rage was so easy to conceal.

But I did not hate only his unconsciousness of me. I remember, too, an exigent need to be free of my life, a need that might have been as urgent no matter what he'd said or done. My work seemed to me unbearably repetitive. Laboriously I made my way upward through the ranks of the faculty. I looked every year for the exceptional student—tried to reach out, to make some sort of contact. I rewrote my lectures. But even so, I was bored.

And you, children, were here. I would not be moved again by the drama, the absorption, of birth and suckling.

Why is it that I cannot lie down like a cat in a patch of sunlight under a south window and purr and be content?

Oh, I want someone else, something else, I said. Is my heart not to be stirred one more time?

Remember I was forty.

I wanted, wanted, wanted, as Henderson said—friendship, adventure, admiration, passion, joy. I wanted you, children, coming in for supper promptly at six, George in his accustomed chair with a child in his lap. I, too, wanted our leafy green-lighted house. I wanted a lover. I wanted it all.

I wanted to be young again.

It was then that I could have taken up with poor old Harry Trent. But, Christ, I wasn't suicidal. I loved Harry, yes, but with very little imaginative effort I could see him on our doorstep at four in the morning, dead drunk, his beautiful long swimmer's body limp as a pile of sticks, howling my name. He did howl sometimes, later, but I could come to the rescue and he could howl, each of us with a clear conscience.

And in that moment of deep frustration, the first paroxism

of grief for vanished youth—my taut skin slackening—she appeared, shouldered her way across the campus against a strong March wind, sandy hair blowing back from her round brow, a saddle of translucent brown freckles across her delicately modeled small nose, her eyes, level and very dark brown, *looking*, as if she meant to see the world and catalogue precisely its every detail.

And, as I was to learn, she did observe; she remembered whether leaves were opposite or alternate on a stem, watched a bird she couldn't identify swing on a wire and afterwards described him accurately, spotted the single four-leaf clover in the grass.

I know you remember them, children, even though they've been gone so long and even though I have never talked about them. That is, I know you remember Judith and David. You didn't see much of Lee.

They came when they did because Lee was available at midterm to take over the courses of an associate professor of history who'd had a heart attack. Judith was teaching photography in the extension program, and of course you and David, Corinne, were in kindergarten together.

We became friends immediately, almost without thought.

She was the adult incarnation of a child I had loved when I was eleven.

There are images, I'm sure, that are printed on the retina in the womb, their outlines filled from time to time by incarnations in the temporal world. They can be as threatening as the shadow of a hawk to a baby chick or can trigger, like the image of the mother hen, all one's need for warmth, food, love, company, can make one follow—without question—over a cliff, into the sea.

A crooked, loving, self-deprecating smile, a slender body, a walk. I see her with one shoulder carried a trifle forward, as if she bucked a strong wind. My first lover walked like that, too.

Do you remember my writing of the fatal summer when I was eleven years old, when I was sent to camp, separated from my mother for the first time since those anguished months of my sister's illness when I was six? Do you remember that I used my homesickness, my heartsick longing for my mother's touch, her kiss, as model for the moments when I had to send my first lover home to his wife, the moments now when I feel my separation from George, whether physical or spiritual, as a rending of myself?

That eleventh summer I met and lost the first friend of my dreams, my ideal companion.

She, too, was slight and sandy-haired, smiled with a shy, self-deprecating—I knew the meaning of the smile, if I didn't know the word—lift of one level blond brow; her nose was small and delicately modeled and saddled with freckles, her dark brown eyes took in every changing shade of the day. She could beat me at tennis, at diving, at everything but riding. We cared most of all about riding and I always out-rode and out-jumped her.

What did we say to each other, how did we establish our passionate friendship? I don't recall a single word we spoke, just that I followed her, chirping like a chick to mama, through long sunny days of riding, swimming, giggling, wrestling, running, climbing.

My heart tinkled like a wind chime: I have a friend! I forgot my own mama as completely as if I'd cut out the part of my brain in which she lived. It was another of those occasions when the ant lion turns into the katydid. I was never homesick again.

The summer ended and she was gone. But her face has stayed in my dreams.

So it happened with Judith.

Sunday Jan. 4th

She created for me a world of absolute acceptance.

If I had said to her, Have I ever told you about my second tonsillectomy? (a dreary, horrid, boring tale), she would have said, No! Tell me. And even if I'd told her twice before, her interest would have been genuine. She listened to me—and I to her—with the kind of sisterly acceptance one gives oneself. Have you noticed that we never tire of repeating things to ourselves—find ourselves boundlessly fascinating? Is that what loving one's neighbor as oneself means?

And not just acceptance. Admiration.

To her I was beautiful, witty, intelligent, desirable above all others. I suppose I fell in love in part out of sheer gratitude. Probably I would do it again.

I didn't care a jot whether any of it was true.

Admire me, appreciate me, our tiny souls cry out. Adore me, lie to me, tell me anything—I'll believe anything you say, if only it's meant to let me know how grand I am.

To do me justice, to open the door a crack and let a little humanity seep back into this creature I've been presenting as me, it's true George was just the opposite, and his reserve may have accounted in part for this insatiable yearning of mine. He might say with his life: I'm here. My presence is evidence of my devotion. But he was never free with words, with praise.

And yet, these past three years, I've heard the murmur of his voice on the telephone when he was talking to the boy— a voice full of tenderness that said in every commonplace word, "You, only you, only you." A voice he never used, never, not even in the earliest days of our marriage, with me.

And when I recall hearing it, I say to myself something

altogether different about George. It was not reserve that kept him silent with me or, when he spoke, gave his voice its matter-of-factness; it was that he would not say what he did not feel.

Oh, the pallbearer, standing through prayers at the funeral, lips closed, head unbowed.

He did have, after all, for someone else, the voice, the passion, the tears. He has them still, but not for me.

True? Who knows? Only George. And would I believe him if he denied it?

There you are, my dears, it can't be helped.

Monday Jan. 5th

I find it almost impossible, you see, to leave the present, my present nuttiness, to leave off thinking about George and go back into that faraway past, *my* past, so far receded now that it seems to me to have happened to someone else.

It occurred to me last night as I was falling asleep that I have left out another possible reason why G. never used his tender passionate voice with me. He always knew that I married him out of exhaustion, out of the desire for children, for a stable life. I did not tell him, but he knew. Early on, he took care to hide himself from me, to seem distant, so that, as Albertine did with Marcel, he would finally capture me by elusiveness, so that I would come to desire most what seemed most unobtainable. And then, as the years passed, he forgot that he had ever employed that strategy; it became not deception, but the habit of deception and finally, at the very moment when it had its most unqualified success, the simple truth.

Reasons! I'm sick to death of reasons. And I haven't been notably successful at ferreting out anybody's reasons with the exception of one imaginary grandmother. Also, I'm parsing George's character as if it were my own. Oh, I could write this all over again, give you a new set of conundrums, without half trying, and it would still all be true. But bear with me a little longer. I am going to tell you the story of Judith's and my love affair; but first I must tell you something that perhaps you have already guessed, and that if I am to stop withholding, I should put down now.

During the years when we were lovers it was essential in my view for George to feel rocked in the secure cradle of his life, to suspect nothing. I knew, if I were forced to choose between her and my children and my children's father, that I would choose them, would give her up, and I had not the least desire to make the choice.

Granted, it sometimes crossed my mind that George knew all about it and was indifferent, that it suited him for me to put my passion and attention elsewhere. But that was a measure of what I felt and had little or nothing to do with him.

In any case, there was never an open revelation between us, and after the affair ended, when she was gone, when, after months of dull pain and guilt and grief and bewilderment and regret, I resolved to go back without reservation into my marriage, the reservation, as it turned out, was there whether I liked it or not. I was trapped by my own deceit. Even though I knew that George and I could never be friends unless I told him what my life had been, I saw that telling him could bring him nothing but useless pain. How could I tell him? How contemptible, impossible, to say: This is what I've been. I have to make you suffer through, accept this knowledge so that you can punish me, forgive me, love me.

In short, what confession would not be tainted by my need to confess?

Besides, he might have left me.

I had built a prison of the beams and boards of my own treachery and bolted it together with the iron clamps of my honor and my need.

But then, at last! the circumstances arose in which I could speak without taint, in which my confession would be useful to him—would be fair. And, shameful (I did not think this part then, but I think it now), in which his own guilt would be the means of binding him to me.

So there you have a new item of information, one that has to change your view of George's behavior. I did, at last, when he said to me, "Yes, I am guilty," say to him, "I am guilty, too."

Freely, as I thought, I freed him to betray me. Go your way, I said, as, years ago, I went mine. It's your turn.

171

Remember when I said that I had alternated between euphoria and anguish like someone on a roller coaster at Coney Island? The euphoria was only in part the result of the breaking of that sexual dam. Even more, far more, it was the result of my own confession. At last I had unburdened myself, opened my heart.

For twenty-three years I had hidden myself from him. For seventeen years, since the end of my affair, I had been absolutely alone. To whom could I speak, if not to George? You, children, were there, of course, but no friend, no peer, to hold out a hand and say, I am listening, sister, fellow traveler, sufferer.

I had lived as if on a featureless desert. I stood in the middle of the desert. Sands stretched away in every direction. Far off on the horizon I could see matchstick telephone poles carrying twisted cables, loops of wire. Yes, it's true, other people communicate with one another. Those lines carry voices, thousands of voices speaking out, shouting their joy, weeping their grief, screeching their rage. But I spoke to no one. No one. I was alone, trapped by myself in the prison of myself. George's fall from perfection, his "sin" against me, crashed into my prison and broke it open. There, in his sin, in his humanity, his fallibility, there, above all, even above the sexual reunion, lay the source of my euphoria.

Later

I was careful. I did not burden him with my past as soon as I discovered his affair. I was far too concerned at that point for him. Remember, I'm talking about George at fifty-seven—my predictable, paternal, conscientious George, who turned his garden, memorized his poems, cherished his children—involved with a twenty-six-year-old college dropout who had narrowly missed going to prison for selling drugs. And remember, too, that he had abandoned surgery only a year or so earlier—had abandoned surgery and suffered the death of his mother. I knew, although he never said so, that he had been able to give up surgery just because his mother died. He would never have handed her such a shock at eighty-three.

So he was staggering along on a rotten plank across who knew what abyss.

At first I told him only that I knew about him and the boy. I was intent, to begin with, on eliminating the possibility of blackmail. Then I watched and waited for weeks; and when I was sure he had chosen and continued to choose the course he was on as freely and sanely as anyone is ever free or sane, I told him about me.

When I did, although he expressed astonishment, he forgave and forgot, or so it seemed to me, almost before I finished speaking. He had only the most tenuous interest in my past. He was absorbed in his own present.

I would punish him for that.

So you see, children, there was no need for me to include George in the lineup of those whom I invited to ask questions. If he reads this record, he'll be reading things he mostly already knows.

I see him plowing through to the end, with his foot drawn in, his face as expressionless as when he's cutting a fishhook from a small finger. He's determined. He's already bared his breast to these blows from my green stone. He's put aside the poems. The dumdum has penetrated his liver and throbs there, flowering like an exploding sky rocket. "Now what?" he says, as he turns the pages. "What will she do to me next?"

"I am the one," he says, looking at me from time to time, as I pace the room and watch him read, "I am the one whom the mad doctor flays alive. It's my bloody carcass on the floor. You have the scalpel."

And sometimes, when he's weary, weary—not just with threading together torn pieces of gut or pumping whisky and Quaaludes from the stomachs of his friends' children and his children's friends, but with confronting me, he'll lay the pages down and think of his lost young admiring companion, of open-hearted hours with him, and close his eyes and will himself to sleep, as if to death.

Wednesday Jan. 7th

Fideau is on his chain, barking like a rabid monster at the Doberman that persists in urinating on his favorite tree.

Do you suppose I believe that if I were to kill Fideau, to blow his brains out, it would release me—and him—from the wicked ogre's spell? That from his bloody corpse would rise my blameless, unblemished prince—my purified George?

Or my purified self?

Thursday Jan. 8th

It began when Judith said without warning one day (we were walking across the campus, had just finished laughing at some silly joke, something one of my students had said), "I've fallen in love with you, Corinne. There it is. It's causing me a lot of pain. I don't think we should see each other anymore."

I suppose I had halfway expected it, although I would never have said the same thing to her, no matter how strongly I felt. I was too passive then, in all matters sexual. And besides, I wouldn't have thought there was the least possibility she would respond. But she didn't think I would either—the difference between us was that she spoke. She was always direct.

As soon as she did, my life turned around. I went through the usual declarations—not of passion, but of affection, friendship—thinking I would end by saying, "But I don't want to lose it—the friendship. Surely . . ." etc. Instead, without knowing I was going to, I said, "Give me three days. Let me think about it."

At the end of three days, I said, "Me, too."

Afterwards . . . What can I say except that we were friends? There is nothing I want to put into that ridiculous Sexual Appendix. We cherished each other, were carnal and spiritual sisters. We lay down together in love and trust.

I went to her often in the morning after the older children left for school, after I dropped you, Corinne, at kindergarten, after George left to make rounds or to operate. She was a free-lance photographer and worked, sometimes for the local paper, sometimes on assignment from UPI, but very often for herself, doing on speculation a story that interested her. She could arrange her time. And that year, because of her, I planned my teaching schedule so that I had at least three free mornings or afternoons a week.

I would drive to her house in the dry, clear morning air on a day in fall when the white-boned sycamores glimmered, when the oak trees lifted their flashing bronze helmets to the sun and the gums had turned every color from plum to gold. My heart would be humming like a new top, like tires humming on a smooth pavement, and I would catch myself opening my eyes wide, as if to take in every corner of the day, saying to myself over and over, "It's all free, all free, all free."

For each of us what wasn't free—the love that entailed responsibility, boredom, misunderstanding, pain—was at home. I drove away from that, toward her, toward cool sunny mornings, starry nights, lived inside a bubble of love.

You see, I was silly at forty, just as I was silly at twenty-four and am silly at sixty-two.

Not very many months passed before nothing was free anymore.

Without words we had agreed together that we would say nothing about our husbands qua husbands. We might betray them, but there would be no trashy exchanging of personal and sexual idiosyncrasies and shortcomings. They were our friends.

We would keep our separate lives in separate compartments.

But Judith's husband, unlike George, was not a man who could be put in a box labeled *Friendship and Silence*, and then be depended on to stay there.

The first evidence of a crack in the box took me by surprise.

It was late spring. Judith and I had been lovers since the past summer, saw each other almost every day.

Let me tell you, children, that in those days in a small city like ours—before marriage became "serial monogamy" and no one cared a tap who slept with whom—one of the advantages of a love affair between women was that no one, *no one*, suspected it was a love affair. Oh, if you were both single and lived together and one of you wore nothing but man-tailored suits and four-in-hand ties and had a man's haircut, there would be discreet and interested murmurs. But if you were both reasonably feminine-looking (and we were), were married, had children, then there would never be even the breath of a question.

While, with a man, my God, what a pain! You couldn't even drive down the street together, couldn't run into each other and have a drink at the Yacht Club without someone saying, "Ah ha!"

The same was not true with two men. Men, of course, were not supposed to have intimate friendships with each other except for the purpose of sitting sprawled in front of the TV set looking at football or creeping around some swamp in the icy winter dark, trying to outthink a flock of ducks. The sight of an older man continuously in the company of a young man was unacceptable to the community. Unless, of course, perfect camouflage, the older man were a coach, the younger a player, the older an alumni sponsor, the younger a star quarterback. In those circumstances, anything goes.

All this had to do, I suppose, with a demographic stability that no longer exists anywhere and with the hold of churches on their congregations. (It used to be, too, that people were destroyed by illicit passion—threw themselves in front of trains or chained themselves to rocks and turned into hedgehogs.)

Nowadays, of course, it's different. The open evidence of passion—any variety—is worn like the Congressional Medal of Honor. It's proof that we're courageous, resourceful, reckless. Everything is forgiven, in the name not of Jesus but of lust. We rise up from fucking and shout, "I must be—Yes! I am— alive!" But at the same time, stuck with our passions—or the lack of them—no system to put them in, we flop around like chickens with our heads cut off, bumping bloodily into each other's warm reflexive bodies.

But to go back to Judith and Lee and George and me, not only did I see her every day but we also had a tenuous "couples" friendship, saw them occasionally at night, invited them over for a drink or for supper. But George and I both found the husband difficult. He was bright, knew his field, could talk about whatever one talks about, but he was one of those people who are friends one night, silent strangers the next. He made George uneasy, made me feel a gripping guilt: Does he suspect? Maybe he knows.

Sometimes, when he worked late at the college or had a departmental meeting, she might come and bring David for an early supper. It was on those nights that she and George became friends. He could talk to her by the hour about the techniques of her profession, liked to look at her pictures, even bought a camera and got her to begin teaching him to work in the darkroom.

One Saturday that first spring, she and I took you children on an all-day picnic to the sand bar on the river—our narrow river that was still green and moving and fishy in those days. We stayed late, looked in the gravel for fossil-bearing rocks. She found a flat stone printed with the delicate outline of a fern leaf. I, as usual, found nothing but an occasional crinoid. We lay for a long time side by side on our blanket, hardly talking, watching you wade in a shallow pool left behind by the spring rise, feeling the warm sand under our bodies, touching hands now and then.

The sun went down and then, at dusk, as they do, the bream began to bite in the failing light and we stayed on, catching fish.

It was dark when we got to Judith's house. Lee was standing in the lighted doorway, motionless, as if he'd been waiting, watching.

I called out to him, "Come see what we've caught," got out of the car and began to untie the poles from their rack.

He continued to stand in the doorway for a moment, then strode down the steps, down the walk toward us, looming out of the darkness, the light behind him, his long shadow preceding him. He was very tall, remember? Six-three probably, dark-haired, heavy-shouldered. I could not see his face clearly, but

I saw against the light that he clenched and unclenched his fists once, as if admonishing himself to self-control. I shivered. He opened the back door of the car without looking at either of us. "Come on, son, get out," he said.

"I caught two fish, Daddy," David said. "You can have them."

You were silent, Corinne, asleep, I think; the boys drowsy.

The light from the interior of the car shone on Lee and David and there was something curiously similar in the expressions on their faces, around their thin, beautifully cut lips. David, slight and blond, looked like Judith, except around the mouth. What was it I saw there? A queer detached smile, meant to ingratiate, as if, for each, the Child behind the mask had suffered excessively and now was crafty, invulnerable.

He turned to Judith. "Where have you been?" he said, still smiling.

"Picnicking. I told you we might . . ."

"You're late, my dear," he said. "You said you'd be home by seven. I don't like you out after dark. Besides, I want my supper."

"We're all right, darling. Nobody would take on this crowd."

"I want my supper."

"All right."

He hadn't spoken to me.

"Hello, Lee. You should have gone with us," I said. "It was a beautiful day."

"I'll take these." He reached out for the fishing poles.

"Look out for the hooks. That one's loose."

He looked at me as intently as if I'd said something significant. That is, his eyes were intent. He still had that disconnected smile on his lips. Then: "Yes," he said. "I see it. I don't miss much."

What in the world?

"I'm going to give you my fish, Daddy," David said again.

"Well," I said, "I reckon we'll be getting along. The children are weary. And George'll be wanting his supper, too. See you both soon."

The next time Judith and I were alone—we were at her house in the kitchen, washing and drying the dishes, and David was at school—she said, "I didn't tell you, I kept putting it off, but Lee has problems off and on."

"Problems?"

"He— Haven't you wondered why we're here? Why we were available at midterm last year, were willing to move down from the University of Michigan to this?"

"Yes," I said, "but . . ." I touched her hand. "You know how we are with each other," I said. "I try to be careful. I don't want to do anything to rock the boat. I want you to be free to come to me, not to have to talk about anything you don't want to talk about. I know you know that." I put down my towel, sat on the stool at the counter. "Besides," I said, "there are so many simple explanations. Maybe you wanted to come to the South. Or . . . I don't know."

"If there had been a simple explanation, I would have given it."

"Yes," I said. "Of course you would have. Maybe I was afraid to get into it."

"He didn't get tenure," she said. "The reason he didn't was not, as you may have heard by the grapevine, because his department head felt threatened by him, but because he flipped out, had to be carted away. When he came back, they didn't want to take him on for life. Too risky." She didn't look at me, kept washing and washing the same small round saucer. "We live a 'highly structured' life," she said, putting the words in quotation marks with her voice. "He finds rigid temporal and spatial structures reassuring. He doesn't like anything out of place—or early or late. As long as we're careful, things go pretty well with us. The other day—when we went fishing— I thought he was reconciled—prepared—for us to be a bit late."

"Of course I know how orderly you always make things," I said. "I supposed it was you."

She looked at the saucer front and back, as if it might be concealing something. I saw that she was controlling tears, reached out to her, drew her to me, put my arms around her, laid my head between her breasts. "Put that silly saucer down," I said.

"It has its pluses," she said, "particularly for David. I think children need structures—need to know what to expect, don't you?"

I nodded against her breast, thinking of David's offer of his fish, so clearly meant to placate his father, of that strange detached smile.

"He loves David," she said.

Again I nodded.

"He's so vulnerable," she said.

I did not say, "David, too." She knew that.

I let her go, stood up. "We'll just have to be more careful," I said. "We can manage." I took the saucer from her. "I'll try to help," I said. "I love you."

And we were careful. From beginning to end we tried to keep him secure and content.

But temporal and spatial structures are fragile and, sane or crazy, you may find—I have found—they won't always, or even often, contain or control your fears and passions.

After that day we talked and talked and talked—about Lee's life and all our lives, about the terrible, irremediable reservations between men and women that make us feel sometimes that we must be different species.

We never believed we had answered any questions. But we continued to weave and elaborate and embroider the fabric of our life together.

At the same time, George and Judith were becoming friends. He had liked her from the beginning, and as time passed, he became more and more interested in talking to her about photography. During the third year he set up a darkroom in the garage; and they both worked there, she during the day, George mostly at night. On his days off he wandered the city with his tripod and a secondhand view camera he'd bought with her guidance in St. Louis. He took pictures of buildings, cityscapes, stark sad pictures of old warehouses, netted in patterns of telephone poles and wires, schoolhouses with abandoned playgrounds, our synagogue, circa 1910, with its curiously Russian-looking onion domes, set down in the middle of a black slum.

Judith thought his pictures good. He had an unerring eye for the frame and was developing his sense of how to use light and shadow. But his choices made me sad. In the playground picture a swing is moving and its blurred passage is recorded on the film. A child may just have jumped down, or the wind may have blown it. In the synagogue picture, there is the shadow of a man in one corner. But mostly the buildings seem to have lost their human inhabitants, who perhaps have left just ahead of the demolition crews.

Later

As for me, I struggled with my hatred. I believed George both deserved and didn't deserve it. But after all, I both felt and didn't feel it.

When I fulfilled my "obligation" to satisfy his lust, it was a kind of civilized rape. How could he rape me under the delusion that he was pleasing me, that all was well between us? Later, when I might have been, I was never so insensitive to him. I *knew*—the instant the boy laid his hand on George's shoulder. I heard that affair in George's voice.

But now, looking back, I have to say this. I set it up. I consented to it. I arranged the continuing life that invited him to rape and permitted me to hate. I drew him close and opened my legs and stared over his shoulder into the darkness—all in the name of stable family life and what was best for the children.

Oh, if only he'd said, "I know. I love you. It doesn't matter. Come back to me"—the words I said later to him—how wholly, how instantly I would have abandoned her, no matter that I loved her, no matter that I felt I'd known her always, in a dozen other lives.

And it was best for you, children, wasn't it? Would some other life have been better?

Friday Jan. 9th

Does it seem to you, reading, that I have been inventing again—in Judith, the ideal companion; in our motives, the purest friendship; in George, the inhuman, cold, blind professional; in Lee, the dark and hulking madman? Perhaps I have.

Does it seem that we had the two men where we wanted them—the unsuspecting victims of our conspiracy?

I can only point out that I, too, have thought of this.

Saturday Jan. 10th

By 1962 things weren't going well for Lee. The darkness was gathering again. She said nothing, but I knew that he had walked up to a colleague on the campus one day, held him by the lapel, and told him not to "shrink away."

"I saw you turn your head and try to avoid me," he said. "It's all right. I know I stink. Everyone is polite and pretends to find nothing offensive about me, but I've always had this same chemical odor about my body—ever since I can remember."

The man did shrink away then. (Do you remember Dr. Halston—a short, elderly fellow with a potbelly like a volley ball?) He danced around Lee on his short, thin legs, saying, "Ho, ho, Lee. Ho, ho," in a voice like a department store Santa Claus's. "I couldn't think of anything to do but laugh," he told me afterwards.

Lee said that he was aware the smell was getting worse. "It's not that I don't bathe," he said. "There's nothing I can do about it."

Through the grapevine I heard about a couple of puzzling scenes with students.

I told Judith what I'd heard. And while I was telling her, I looked at her and realized that she was haggard, weary.

"I have to tell you what I know," I said. "I think you need to know it, too."

"Oh, I know," she said. "I know already. How could I not?"

It was late March. We were sitting on the slope of the levee behind the house watching you and David, Corinne, trying to get a kite up. No matter how fast you ran with it, the wind would take it up fifty feet and then drop it into the grass. The slope of the levee was red with clover bloom, an intricate tapestry of green and crimson. Judith began to pull the flowers and loop and tie the stems into a chain. I watched her hands. I loved to watch her hands, small and strong and competent, stained with darkroom chemicals.

She said, "He's seeing Dr. Cromer. Do you know him?"

I shook my head, no.

"I don't know," she said. "He seems sensible. He put Lee back on the medicine again—he'd stopped taking it for a while. But he's getting worse." She tied another flower into the chain and another and another, silent. "I may have to divorce him," she said. "I'm worried about David. But I can't abandon Lee. I can't. And . . ." She reached out to me, took my hand, drew the loops of clover over my wrist like a bracelet. Then: "Look," she said, separating a mound of clover leaves by my knee, "here's a four-leaf. We need it." She laid it in my hand.

"If I do," she said, "—leave him, I mean—I think I would —that I ought to leave." She looked straight at me under level blond brows, calm, clasping her strong stubby fingers in her lap. "Leave you," she said.

"*What?* You need me. Under those circumstances you'll need me even more."

"It's no way to raise a child."

"We're always careful," I said.

She shook her head, looking down now at her clasped hands. "Corinne, you *know* . . ."

"I couldn't bear it," I said. "I can't do without you." And, when she didn't answer: "What can we do that isn't wrong for someone for one reason or another?"

She stared out over the slope of the levee at the red-winged blackbirds darting and flying at the water's edge, calling to each other in liquid voices, their shoulder patches brighter than the clover blooms.

The children were far away, the kite high above the trees at last.

"I'm pregnant," she said.

"Judith! Why didn't you tell me?"

"I haven't been sure. I'm still not sure. I'm only two weeks late. But I'm never late, you know, and I was sickish this morning. I haven't even told Lee."

I was sick with rage. I never thought about her in bed with Lee. I had a box to put that in: She, too, had to acquiesce in rape. She suffered him without feeling, without a twinge of lust. But—pregnant? The box splintered and he came climbing out.

And then—the possibility that she might leave me. Christ, you know all that: the rock resting on my chest, so that I had to draw deep breaths to keep from suffocating, the lines of pain from my belly to my ribs. It all happened again as if for the first time.

To whom would she go? Would she find another lover? Would she suffer? It would be better for her to die than to leave me.

Besides, I cared about her, about her predicament and her pain.

I tried to gather my thoughts.

"What about David?" I said. "What do you mean, you're worried about him?"

"Lee doesn't like David anymore. He just doesn't like him."

"He hasn't liked him for a long time," I said. "He doesn't like anybody."

"Oh, Corinne, we can't talk about him as if he were normal. We can't be angry with him. Something new is going on in his head about David. Whatever it is, I have to protect David. And now—this. I've been thinking about an abortion, but I can't bring myself to it. Everything in me says, No. Out of the question." Her voice was low, sensible.

I pulled the loops of clover off my wrist, began to tear the flowers apart. "I hate him," I said.

"Well, don't," she said. "It's a waste of energy. I know I have to separate our lives from his," she went on. "The children's and mine, I mean."

"I'm sorry," I said. "I shouldn't have said that."

"Corinne, I'm afraid of him."

"Afraid? What's he done to you?"

"Nothing—yet. This time. Just—almost. Oh, I feel so sad for him."

"My God, if you're afraid—Christ, you have to get out."

"I've been afraid of him before," she said.

It was as if she opened a door to me that she had never opened before, showed me a dark receding corridor, winding back into her past, forward into her future. Afraid? How could you tolerate even for one day a life with a man you feared? What kind of love courted violence, invited a blow from that dark powerful man?

"In practical terms," she went on in her gentle sensible voice, "suppose I leave him. How am I going to manage for the next year or two? I can work almost until the baby comes. But then, afterwards—I think I can manage, but money will be tight."

I hated her voice when she was calm and sensible. But for Christ's sake, what did I want? If I had gotten pregnant . . .

I stop and think about it, try to remember what I thought underneath what I said.

If I had gotten pregnant, I would have left her. I couldn't have carried a child and gone on with the affair, it would have gone against my deepest, most uncontrollable feelings—and I knew it. Without a thought, I knew it.

"It's crazy to talk about leaving," I said. "I mean, leaving here, me." You can't leave me, somebody inside me was screaming hysterically. It's out of the question. I'll kill him. I'll cut off his head with an ax.

But at the same time somebody else was saying, Oh, George, my gentle, disciplined, sane George, my sensible George, where are you? I've seen you stitch your own child's torn lip with stitches so tiny, a hand so steady that afterwards the scar vanished within six months. How did I leave you? How did I get into this mess?

188

"George and I can help you make it work," I said. I felt as if my head were up there with the kite, tugging away at the string, ready to burst, to fly off into the sun. I said, calmly, "First I think we—George, maybe, with Dr. Cromer's help— need to persuade Lee . . ."

"He hasn't flipped out yet," she said. "I would never, never hospitalize him again, except as an absolute last resort."

"But, if you're afraid of him . . ."

"I think I have to risk leaving him," she said. "When I try to decide what's best for everybody, I say to myself that it's not just me and David. It may be that I'm the worst possible person for Lee. Maybe he'd make a new contact with the world, if he were alone, if we went away. And *you.*" She shrugged. "Who knows? In any case, it's obvious the sensible thing for me would be to go back to Dayton to Mama, home. I can live at home for a limited while, until after the baby comes. And then—it's not that I couldn't support them. I could."

"No," I said. "No."

Here's a possibility that has always haunted me. Maybe I didn't love Judith at all. Maybe I loved only her love for me. Maybe I'm a monster, incapable of love.

Except for you, children. I love you. I do. I do.

She put off telling him she was pregnant for another month, put off leaving him—and leaving me.

One day he appeared without explanation or appointment in George's office and demanded to see him. This, of course, was long before George went into emergency medicine, when he still had an office, kept appointments, did X tonsillectomies, X hysterectomies, X appendectomies every year. He had the usual screen of receptionist and office nurse to speed him through the day as efficiently as possible. When the receptionist asked Lee if he had an appointment, he shook his head.

"I have plenty of time," he said. "I'll wait."

"The doctor usually sees patients through referrals," she said. "If you have a problem, perhaps you should see your internist first. Or . . . ?" She waited for him to explain what he wanted, a question in her voice.

"I'll wait," he said again. He crossed the office, sat down in the heavy armchair opposite her desk. The springs creaked. The legs splayed a fraction of an inch. He continued to look at her.

I suppose she saw something unusual in his eyes, heard a threat in the creaking chair.

"He was so big," she told George afterwards.

He had not said he was a friend, had said nothing but, "I'll wait." When George finished with the patient he was examining, she told him that Lee was waiting.

After he heard what Lee had to say, George canceled the rest of his appointments, came home in the middle of the afternoon, and told me what had happened.

Now, I can put myself without effort into Lee's place. Not

that I would have been so crazy as he was. But I know how easy
it is to assign a part however one chooses, to whomever one
chooses. I recognize him in myself.

I imagine him those spring nights at home, walking through
his silent house, turning on the television set, trying to watch
the late movie, tiptoeing into his bedroom, staring down at
Judith, sniffing the air, while Judith, sunk in her pregnant
dreams, feels in her sleep the nipples draw, senses in the changing presence of her room his anguish, his rage, turns on her side
and stirs, draws up her knees to cradle and shield the unborn
child.

He goes to David's room and looks down at him sleeping,
face down on his narrow child's bed, one arm flung out, hand
trailing. His straight blond hair falls in a neat cap around his
ears, the back of his frail neck is visible between hair and
T-shirt. His face is turned toward Lee, his mouth relaxed, his
fearful eyes closed. He is caught up, perhaps, in a dream of
invulnerable fortresses, invincible long bows and javelins and
broadswords.

He might be Judith's child alone, the product of partheno-
genesis.

Poor Lee, he cannot be at peace. Even in their sleep they
are deceiving him, laughing at him, plotting against him.

He brushed past the nurse, George said, strode into the
office, and loomed over him—two hundred and fifty pounds of
anger.

George stood up and I feel sure he stepped back. He cannot
bear to have his space violated. Probably he put out his hand
in greeting. "Lee!"

"She hasn't told me she's pregnant. I suppose you are aware
of that."

"What?"

"Just because I'm surrounded by the odor—oh, I'm sure
she's discussed that with you, hasn't she? She wouldn't leave
me a shred of privacy. But just because of that, you needn't
think I've lost my own sense of smell. I know. I've always been

able to . . . I have this uncanny, abnormal sense of smell."

"Sit down, Lee," George said. "Sit down, man. I'm not sure what you're talking about. Sit down and start over again. OK? I'm listening."

"—always been able to— Most people, I suppose, can smell a woman, no matter how clean she is, and know she's in her period, but I can smell pregnancy. Not many people can do that."

What George thought immediately was that Lee thought—indeed, that he might have reason to think—he had a brain tumor. As soon as he heard "abnormal sense of smell," the surgeon in him sat up and took notice.

"Hang on a minute there," he said. "You're going a little bit too fast for me. OK?" He made his voice a shade sterner, as he does to control an almost hysterical patient. (And what would be more likely to drive a strong, healthy, forty-year-old man to hysteria than the conviction that he has something malign growing inside his skull?) "Sit down, Lee. Tell me about it."

"Tell *you* about it! You know. What is there for me to tell you about it? You tell me."

"You've been smelling something unusual? What kind of odor?"

"Don't think I haven't gone over our lives. I've worked out the calendar. Nine and a half years ago, right? I remember very well it was in June of '54 that . . ."

"Nine years! Lee, you're going way too fast for me," George said. "I realize you're upset, you're anxious, but it's more than likely we've got a harmless situation here, something we can eliminate or control. And the longer you tell me it's been going on and you've stayed in good health, the more likely that's true. All right? But there isn't any way for me to find out what's wrong with you unless you answer my questions sensibly. Sit down!"

Lee crossed the office to the open window, pounded twice on the windowsill with his closed fist, turned, crossed the office again, looked at George's framed diplomas on the wall, came back, sat down in the patient's chair by the desk, looked at George. "What did you say?" he said.

"I said I have to ask you about your symptoms."

("He smiled at me," George said later to me, "like a crafty child, like a clown.")

What he said was: "Of course. I might have guessed how you would try to handle it. But I won't allow it. You'll never get me that way. Now listen: There's nothing wrong with me. *She's* pregnant."

"Who's pregnant?" George said.

"I've gone over our lives together. I've studied the calendar. It was in 1954 that she got the AP assignment to travel in the South, do the photographs for a series on Southern reactions to *Brown* v. *Board of Education*. Remember? Of course you do. She didn't tell me she was here. She would never have mentioned that, would she? You're both too clever to make that kind of slip. You bide your time and wait. You see each other . . . Where? I wouldn't have any trouble working it out with Corinne, would I? Would either of you even care if I asked Corinne? We could go over the seminars together, the conventions, her assignments . . .

"But I won't do that. I'm decent enough to leave Corinne out of it.

"And then—four years ago—to maneuver me into taking the job here! To take it up right under my nose . . ."

"Lee, are you talking about your wife? Do you think Judith is pregnant?"

"That's the laugh of the century." He stood up, that huge dark bitter driven man in his imaginary bubble of chemical odors through which the real odor of Judith's pregnancy had penetrated, a needle of reality, and leaned his head against the wall of George's office, laid his hand on the framed diploma, pointed to the date George passed the surgical boards as if it had a mystical significance, and wept. When he sat down again, the chair by George's desk creaked under him as if it might split under the burden of his anguish.

"My son," he said. "My boy. David. My son is not my son.

And now another child. She is going to have another child of yours."

"Lee," George said, "I am not involved with your wife. Not in any way. I never saw her in my life until Corinne brought her to the house four years ago."

"And you sit there, lying, looking at me as if you can make me think I'm crazy. But that's all part of it, along with laying the groundwork for telling me I've got a brain tumor. Do you think I'd go under *your* knife?" He got up again. "I'm leaving," he said. He was out the door, had slammed it behind him before George could speak. Three long steps across the waiting room, looking neither to left nor to right and he was gone. George followed him out of the building, calling to him, but he got in his car and drove away.

George said all he could think about was Judith and the child. What to do about them.

And I? As he told me, I sat silent, unable to think.

"I called her as soon as I saw him drive off," George said, "but her phone didn't answer."

I gathered my wits. "He might kill them," I said. "Or you. He's crazy. Judith told me he was getting crazy again."

"Again?" George said.

"He had a breakdown—a schizophrenic episode—several years ago, before they came here."

But before we did anything, the telephone rang and it was Judith. She had picked David up at school and taken him to play with a friend. "I knew already I couldn't risk bringing him to you," she said. "Christ! George! He thinks George is David's father, the father of this child."

"I know," I said.

"I didn't know it until noon today, when he came home from the college with George on his mind. It's my fault, Corinne, all my fault. I should have left a month ago. I should have gone, I couldn't bear to leave you, that's what it was. I couldn't bear it."

"George is here, Judith," I said. "We'll come over." I had

to warn her to be careful what she said. But it may be, too, that I was scrambling for cover.

So, my dears, that was how it all ended. Ended in days, weeks, of nightmare, trying to persuade him that his belief about the affair was an illusion, trying to get him to commit himself, taking turns listening to his nonstop tirades, trying to get him into a hospital, and then trying to get him to stay there.

Does it sound like a soap opera? Well, too bad if it does. I can't do anything about that.

When he was gone, she sold her house, gathered herself together, left.

Everyone knows what it's like to lose a mate, a beloved friend. I felt as if someone had thrown a rock at me, struck me in the temple, when I was riding an escalator. I had to keep moving with the moving stairs. I staggered, scrambled to keep myself upright, hung onto the side rail. Some days I didn't care if I got to the top and went through the crack and never came out. I got up, attended to the children's needs, George's needs, taught, and went to bed, careened through my life.

Judith didn't divorce him right away. He came out of that episode in three or four months and she didn't file for divorce until he was settled in a new job. I heard through one of the men in his department that he was teaching in a high school in a small town in Georgia.

To begin with, Judith wrote me occasionally. It would have been too strange, too noticeable to George, if we hadn't made a pretense of keeping up with each other. She said that he was settled, and then, after a year, that they were divorced. Later that year she wrote that she was still with her parents, but that she was ready to go back to work, to get an apartment, try to put together a peaceful life for her children.

Four years afterwards she remarried. By that time we had stopped writing. I was besieging George's citadel again. I never met her second husband.

I wish for her that she has in him such a friend as she was to me.

But David.

When he was sixteen or so, he, too, appeared one day in George's office, thin and anxious and determined. He, too, asked the question Lee had asked: Are you, is it possible that you are my father?

"I would rather have you for a father," he said, "than him. He hated me."

"I wanted to take him out and buy him steaks and ice-cream cones," George told me afterwards. "Judith's straight look—you know—made me feel so sad."

George sat him down and shook his head and talked to him quietly, said to him, "No, son, no, you wouldn't rather have me. You wouldn't.

"He didn't hate you," he said. "Some damaged, unloved part of him hated you, just as some damaged part of you hates him. Do you understand that? And you don't want me for a father. You haven't thought what it would mean if I were your father. It would mean that I had never acknowledged you, that I had let your mother fight all her battles alone, that I was a coward and a scoundrel, a loveless egoist . . . You see?

"And I am not. I have never so much as laid my hand on your mother's arm, looked at her with desire as she walked away from me. She was my friend, my wife's friend. That's all. And your father . . ."

But what could he say about Lee?

"Try not to judge him," he said.

Afterwards I thought the boy's motivation in seeking George out might as easily be love for Lee as hate. *After all*, he might say to himself, *if George were my father, my physical father, then he* (Lee) *would have been justified in his anguish, his rejection of me. It would have been understandable, forgivable.*

He spent the night with us, a frail, underfed blond lad—a straight look, 'yes, but that crafty smile still on his lips. He had no interest in me.

I wrote to Judith that he had come and gone and she wrote back that he had quit school, wandered in and out of their lives, sometimes had a job, sometimes lived in a commune, supported by his friends.

He wandered that flowery world, that sad world, all through the early seventies, and then, she wrote me, he settled down, went to college, got a degree. He was planning to marry, she said.

Now, I suppose, like the rest of us, he struggles to hold his life together.

Saturday Jan. 17th

The letters.

George's letters from the boy he loves. I have to go back to them.

I never stopped looking for them.

Nothing about that is straight or clear. But I have to tell you the rest.

I have been reading Troyat's biography of Tolstoy. As all the world knows, Tolstoy died of pneumonia in the stationmaster's house at Astapovo, a small rural railroad station hundreds of miles from his villa. At eighty-two, he had run away from his wife of forty-eight years, who had borne him twelve children, devoted her life to him, tormented him with her jealousy. He would become a Tolstoyan monk, a contemplative, a solitary, a follower of himself.

In his diary a few days before he left home he wrote: "My relations with Sonya are becoming more and more difficult. What she feels for me is not love, but the possessiveness of love, something that is not far from hatred and is being transformed into hatred. The children saved her before. An animal love, but full of self-denial. When that was over, there remained only intense egoism. And egoism is the most abnormal state of all, it is insanity . . ."

But she knew that he had disinherited her and their children, had left all he possessed to support his Tolstoyan communes.

Of her husband's love for his secretary, Chertkov, which she believed to be sexual and he declared to be pure, Sonya wrote: "I feel like killing Chertkov, or sticking something into his bloated body to release the soul of Leo Nikolayevich from his deleterious influence."

"Cursed by my daughter," she wrote, "rejected by my husband . . ."

Of disinheriting his sons, Tolstoy wrote: ". . . one cannot deprive millions of people of what is necessary to their souls . . . in order that Andrey may drink and carry on and Leo scribble books."

But the next day he wrote of the secretary he loved, who had moved him to this radical act: "Chertkov has involved me in a conflict that is painful and repellent to me . . ."

When she understood that he had left her forever, the sixty-eight-year-old Sonya threw herself into the lake at Yasnaya Polyana. When she was dragged out of the water and left alone in her room, she jabbed herself with scissors, with a knife, with pins, beat her breast with a paperweight, a hammer.

He wrote to her from the monastery where he spent a few nights: "Do not suppose that I left you because I don't love you. I do love you and I pity you with all my soul, but I have no choice . . ."

After her attempts to kill herself, Sonya wandered blindly through the house, clutching to her bosom a little pillow that her husband used to put under his cheek. "Dear Lyovochka, where is your thin little head lying now?" And then hissed between clenched teeth: ". . . savage beast! He tried to kill me!"

"Lyovochka," she wrote, "awaken the love that is in you and you will see how much love you will find in me . . . I embrace you, my dear, my old friend, who loved me once . . . Well, God keep you, take care of yourself."

At the last, insane with grief, she prowled outside the house where he lay, tried to peer in the windows. She was not permitted to go to him. Her daughter covered the windows with blankets.

Inside, Tolstoy asked how she was, where she was, wept. "Tell me! Tell me!" he said. "What can be more important than that?"

In a moment of lucidity he said, "Much has fallen upon Sonya."

She had been one of his models for the young girl Natasha in *War and Peace,* irresistibly vital, charming, generous-hearted, courageous; for the earth mother Natasha in the final pages, surrounded by husband and children, an infant at her breast; and for Anna in *The Kreutzer Sonata,* who is murdered by her husband.

His last words were "The truth . . . I care a great deal . . . How they . . ."

When he was unconscious, dying, she was allowed to approach his bed. She knelt, kissed his forehead, said, "Forgive me, forgive me." But he did not hear.

Monday Jan. 19th

I found the letters. I was right. They—or at least the two I found—were in my house. The affair was still—or again—going on.

In each case I found the letter the day after he received it and read it and answered it.

Where he had put them and what he said afterwards to me still baffle me.

But don't think for a moment that finding them, reading them, plumbing the slimy bottom of my own character, finding out something strange and new about his, set me upon a new path. If the circumstances were to arise again, so uncontrollable is my obsession, I know I would look again, read again, and then—still—stay here in this house with him, continue to try to capture his soul, until some new katydid (maybe a butterfly this time?) crawled out of her shell, abandoned it, and flew off to a new life.

In each case he tore the letter into a number of pieces and put it in the trash basket in our bedroom.

In each case I fished the pieces out of the trash basket, got the Scotch tape, and put it together.

Other people are nobler than I. Other people use their wills to produce the acts that form their lives. Other people *leave* —rather than wallow in their own weakness, their own treachery, their own ruin. I know this is true. I have seen them do it. I have read about them in books. I have invented and dreamed other lives for myself.

Tuesday Jan. 20th

In the middle of the weeks of that search—before I found the letters, when I knew that George knew I was looking, when I could not stop looking—I stood up in my empty kitchen one afternoon and screamed as loud as I could scream.

Screaming, as you know, is a technique recommended by many schools of therapy for relieving tension. As you also know, our house is set far back in its yard in the curve of the levee. There is no chance a neighbor might hear me and be alarmed and rush to my rescue.

But ten minutes later, like Tarzan answering Jane's yodel from another part of the forest, a visitor from out of town came swinging through the trees and landed on my doorstep, a visitor whose name and history are not in any way relevant to this record.

It was then that I had the abortive one-night stand I mentioned—when was it? let's see—on September 8. It was an experiment undertaken—like a course of laetrile or coffee enemas for the desperate terminal cancer patient—to discover whether I might not thus detach myself from my obsession, shrink the malignant tumor that was eating the cells of my soul.

He was and is a sweet fellow, a longtime friend. He was astonished, delighted, unquestioning at this unexpected gift from me. But unfortunately it didn't work.

Later

After I found the first letter I said nothing. For a day it lay untouched in the bottom of the trash basket. I would wait until

George had a twenty-four-hour shift at the hospital to retrieve it.

That night I lay awake hour after hour. I thought I could not wait until the next day to see it. I got out of bed and crossed the room and stared into the trash basket, as if the fragments, inscribed in radioactive ink, might glow, reveal themselves to me, burn my eyeballs in punishment, blind me.

Behind me he stirred and turned over. As I turned toward him, he opened his eyes, looked at me, closed them again without speaking.

I wandered the house, went outside, walked around and around the yard to tire myself out, walked up on the levee, gazed out over the sluggish, reeking river, went finally to the living room and lay sleeping and waking there.

He got up before six the next morning and set out for the hospital. I pretended I was asleep. The day was Friday, the day I empty all the trash baskets in the house for the weekly round of the garbage collector. I could retrieve the letter and empty the trash and the trash would be gone from the garbage can before he came home. My guilt was such that I thought he might check the trash when he got home to see if the letter was still where he had thrown it. And my shame was such that I could not bring myself to piece the letter together there in my own house.

I found a roll of Scotch tape, gathered the fragments I had retrieved, got into the car, and drove to the nearest mall. There, in the concrete desert, surrounded by empty cars and wandering strangers, I put the letter together and read it. Then I took it to my office and put it in an envelope and filed it in a three-drawer steel filing cabinet among back tax records and copies of old examinations and class rolls. Even though I had been ashamed to piece it together in my home—George's home—I could not bring myself to throw it away. I was afraid I would not then be sure it had ever existed.

I decided I would test George.

"Tell me," I said again. "I know it's true. Please tell me."

"No," he said. "It isn't true."

That was the day when, if ever I were to leave him, I would have left. He didn't care if I was crazy. Maybe he even wanted me to be crazy. Is that possible?

The following week he received another and read it and answered it and tore it up. I retrieved it and pieced it together and read it. I said nothing.

Later still

I will not tell you what the letters said, except that they bore out what I knew to be true. But here are some passages they might have contained, words that would have been most devastating to me, words that I imagine might have found their way into other letters, other conversations.

"I was talking to X and X the other day about our situation and your predicament with Corinne and they said, just as they already had to you, that . . ."

"It's the same with me. To get away—away from responsibility, boredom, making do, to a world where everything is free . . ."

"We understand each other so well without a word passing between us, and that's the great . . ."

"No, you mustn't leave her. Don't talk about leaving her, George. You know you don't hate her. You care about her. You've told me so—no matter how dull, how maddening, your life together may sometimes seem. And you know we can't ever make a life together. I have to think about my kids."

"It's OK with me if you find somebody else there to fuck. Especially if it makes it easier for you to manage at home . . ."

"I can't help worrying about Corinne. It's all very well for you to say you fuck her once a week and keep her docile, but . . ."

But all that is only in my relentless imagination. I could make up more and more explicit fictional letters from the puppet boy in my head who must have so little connection with the real man in the real world, letters that would express even more fully all my murderous rage and frustration and hate. I could put them in the Sexual Appendix I've been promising you; but I have decided, after all, not to put in a Sexual Appendix. I have no heart for explicit sexual revelation—of imaginary or of real behavior. Besides, there are more than enough books on these subjects. You, too, can read *The Joy of Sex* and *The Story of O.* and *My Secret Life.* Or you can forget about reading. Like me, you must have more than enough to do containing the floods of passion and fantasy that imagination, unbidden, continues to pour out.

Wednesday Jan. 21st

Some bony splinter of honor at the bottom of my soul cried out against my abandonment of myself. Two days later I made my pot of coffee and sat down in the living room and he drew in his foot and I said, "George, I know. I have read his letters."

And he sighed, looked at me without surprise, without expression, and said, "I cannot give him up. I can't."

Again he said, "Corinne, it has nothing to do with you. Nothing." Said again, "I love you."

But then he said to me something so curious, so baffling, I have not been able to think of even a shred of explanation. It's not like the word *Suicide* by his grandmother's name in the roll book, a word that could have any one (A, B, C, D,) of a number of explanations, but something for which so far I have been unable to think of any plausible—bearable—explanation.

"I tore them up and put them there on purpose for you," he said.

"What?"

"I could have flushed them down the toilet. That's what I usually did with his letters."

"My God, George, why? Why did you do that to me? Do you hate me so much?"

"I thought if you needed to see them badly enough to get them out of the trash and piece them together, then I ought to give you the chance to do it."

"Jesus Christ, why not tell me? All I ever asked was that you be straight with me."

"I don't know," he said. "I don't know why I did it."

There are, after all, A's and B's and C's and D's.

A. He wanted my humiliation, my moral collapse to be complete.

B. His impulse, if misguided, was in some weird way that arises out of his own secretive nature an unselfish one, meant to allow me to know and to pretend, if I wished, not to know.

C. He didn't know what he was doing. *He's* crazy.

D. All of these.

In any case, not long afterwards the boy broke off with him again. So far as I know (but I don't *know* anything), they have not patched it up. George went through another period of anguish, poor fellow, staggering along as if someone had hit him in the head with a rock when he was riding up an escalator.

He's doing better now. He smiles at me again across the card table. We lie together in the winter darkness and he moves his hand along my back, over the curve of my buttocks, draws me to him, twines his legs with mine.

We still lie to each other.

Did you know that some psychological study or other proves statistically that the average human being tells between twenty-three and one hundred and thirty-seven lies a day?

Our life together continues along its mysterious course.

Thursday Jan. 22nd

I awakened last night from a dream of which all that was left was a voice in my head saying, "Where art rules, the artifact is a source of power."

Of course. Isn't that what the Senoi are doing with their found objects and their artifacts made to recall to them the gifts their dream spirits give them?

I am not, then, confessing, not at all, not making myself known, but creating an object that will wield power, children, George, over your imaginations, will transform and distort your lives.

Can it be that instead of love I am insatiable only for power?

That voice in my head, I remembered later, was no part of me, but the voice of Frederick Karls in his biography of Conrad. I had been ready to claim as my own so neat an aphorism, but I can't.

Friday Jan. 23rd

We had our days, our nights, children—when you were small, and later, when all of you were gone.

I see you, George, dozing on a summer Sunday afternoon. I lie down beside you on the old daybed in the living room— so narrow we have to hang on to each other to keep from falling off.

A Chopin nocturne is rippling through the house like the green moonlight of a summer night. We fall asleep together there, as if the music were weaving a net around us, bearing us up, joining us in dreams.

I remember the year—was it '72? the Perseids came, thick as rain, as they did the year the stars fell. I used to hear my grandmother talk of how her grandmother dated things by the year the stars fell.

You weren't at home, any of you, children—must all have gone your individual ways—visiting grandparents, at camp, or at summer school. I don't recall.

But he and I were alone together for a few days in the late summer, and the night of the heaviest rain of stars we took our sleeping bags up the slope of the levee behind the house and spent most of the night there—like children camping out.

The showers were to come between twelve and three and we went out at midnight, taking with us a bottle of wine and cheese and crackers—for no such occasion is complete without a sacred meal. Hot as it was, we built a little low fire of driftwood—sacred, too—and lay watching the streams of meteorites whirling out of a mysterious, lightless vortex ("Comets weep and Leonids sing") as if the void were creating light. They traversed the skies in a widening cone, shooting across fields of stars and dropping earthward like stones of light from a cosmic sling.

When the sky was turning gray we dragged ourselves home, slept till noon, made love in the daylight under the droning fan, with the bedroom door open—alone in the house, as we so seldom were during those years.

Some mysterious unspoken pledge must have been born of the showers of stars. We were friends and lovers for a long while afterwards.

Nowadays we play double solitaire in the evenings as we always have. We've learned a new version we both like. Later we lie in bed, half asleep, warm affectionate leg touching leg —or spoon-fashion against the cold. He says he loves me. I'm filled with desire . . . My heart is broken. So is his.

Perhaps we should go our separate ways. But where should we go? Should we leave our caladiums, our grassy bricks, our green-lighted and breezy house?

Later

And now I'm thinking again of you, children. Again I think of destroying this record, leaving—for you to puzzle over after I'm dead—only some cryptic impenetrable scrawled word like the *Suicide* beside your great-grandmother's name.

Last time you were here in my dreams, James, you put the green stone in my lap; and you, Corinne and William— I put words of anger and impatience against me in your mouths.

Now it's as if all of you are here with me again in this room, around the dying fire of a late winter evening.

You look at one another and at me. You reach out to me . . .

"Never mind your motives, Mama," one of you says. It doesn't matter which one speaks, for it seems to me that you are acting as one. "Never mind your character or, for that matter, ours, or Daddy's. What can we do, any of us, except reach out to one another, stay within reach?"

Ah, children, ah, George, here I am, then, and here is this. Waking and dreaming, I reach out to you all.

ABOUT THE AUTHOR

ELLEN DOUGLAS (a pen name for Josephine Haxton) has written four earlier novels and a volume of short stories. Her first novel, *A Family's Affairs*, and her collection of stories, *Black Cloud, White Cloud*, were each in turn selected by the *New York Times* for inclusion among the ten best fiction titles of the year. Her third novel, *Apostles of Light*, was nominated for a National Book Award, and her fourth, *The Rock Cried Out*, was written under a grant from the National Endowment for the Arts.

Ellen Douglas is married, has three sons, lives in Greenville, Mississippi, and is a writer-in-residence for one semester each year at the University of Mississippi.